By ANDREW GREY

Accompanied by a Waltz
Crossing Divides
Dominant Chord
Dutch Treat
Fire and Water
A Heart Without Borders
In Search of a Story
North to the Future
One Good Deed
Shared Revelations
Stranded • Taken
Three Fates (Anthology)
To Have, Hold, and Let Go
Whipped Cream
Work Me Out (Anthology)

HOLIDAY STORIES

Copping a Sweetest Day Feel • Cruise for Christmas
A Lion in Tails • Mariah the Christmas Moose
A Present in Swaddling Clothes • Simple Gifts
Snowbound in Nowhere • Stardust

ART SERIES

Legal Artistry • Artistic Appeal • Artistic Pursuits • Legal Tender

BOTTLED UP STORIES

The Best Revenge • Bottled Up • Uncorked • An Unexpected Vintage

BRONCO'S BOYS

Inside Out • Upside Down

THE BULLRIDERS

A Wild Ride • A Daring Ride • A Courageous Ride

BY FIRE SERIES

Redemption by Fire • Strengthened by Fire • Burnished by Fire • Heat Under Fire

CHEMISTRY SERIES

Organic Chemistry • Biochemistry • Electrochemistry

Published by DREAMSPINNER PRESS
http://www.dreamspinnerpress.com

Published by DREAMSPINNER PRESS
http://www.dreamspinnerpress.com

A Foreign RANGE

ANDREW GREY

Dreamspinner Press

Published by
Dreamspinner Press
382 NE 191st Street #88329
Miami, FL 33179-3899, USA
http://www.dreamspinnerpress.com/

A Foreign Range
Copyright © 2012 by Andrew Grey

Cover Art by Reese Dante   http://www.reesedante.com

ISBN: 978-1-61372-550-4

Printed in the United States of America
First Edition
June 2012

eBook edition available
eBook ISBN: 978-1-61372-551-1

To Mary Calmes, Amy Lane, and Ariel Tachna.

Chapter One

WILSON EDWARDS walked up the long driveway toward the house he'd just purchased. "Isn't this great?" he asked with a huge smile on his face. He could already feel the tension leaching out of his body. Greenish-brown grass stretched out to the Wyoming mountains, and as far as he could see, there wasn't a house, a car, or any evidence of another human being. In fact, the only thing he could hear was the wind rushing past his ears, and that was perfect. Trees and fences dotted the horizon, but mostly what he saw was land, land, and more land.

"No," Howard said sullenly from next to him. "It's dirty and there's nothing here." Howard somehow made his opinion sound like a pronouncement from God. "Willie, let's get out of here and find a decent hotel, preferably one with a bar."

Wilson whirled on the other man, balling his fists in sharp impatience. "Willie doesn't exist here. He's someone you made up to sell records ten years ago, and I'm really sick of Willie. I'm tired, Howard, and if I hear another crowd chanting my name right now, I'll wring your neck. I need a vacation, and this is where I'm going to take it." Wilson looked down at his manager in total exasperation. Howard was in worn cowboy boots, old-looking jeans, and even an old leather jacket. Well, actually, every stitch of Howard's clothes was very nearly new, just made to look old. It was a costume, just like the clothes Wilson wore. They were cut and made to look Western because that went with his image, but the clothes came from an exclusive shop on Rodeo Drive that made everything to Wilson's measurements, as opposed to the dry goods store or the JCPenney, where real people bought their clothes. "I don't want my life to be fake any longer." Wilson continued walking up the drive, ignoring Howard as he huffed behind him.

"Couldn't we at least have driven up here?"

Wilson looked over his shoulder. "No. I want to actually see the place," he snapped before turning back to look at the small ranch house. Someone had obviously taken care of it because even the shrubs around the house were neatly trimmed, and the house was painted. The barns and stables looked in good repair. Not that he'd really know, but things didn't look dilapidated or run-down. "It's perfect," Wilson said softly, a little more of the underlying tension leaving his body. For months, his back had ached from hotel beds and sleeping on a rolling bus as it moved from one city to another, but all that seemed to leave him as his lungs sucked deep and hard on the clean, fresh air. Wilson's mind settled and cleared as he got closer to what was going to be his home.

"It's a dump," Howard mumbled from behind him.

"I know it isn't Los Angeles, with its houses in the hills, swimming pools, movie stars," Wilson sang from the *Beverly Hillbillies* theme.

"How long do you intend to stay here before you come home?" Howard asked as Wilson stepped onto the empty front porch. Its new owner could see it decorated with a rocking chair and comfortable furniture.

"Howard, the house in Malibu has been sold, and the house in Brentwood is on the market. I'm done with that rat race and all the fake people living in fake Mediterranean houses on streets that look more like Hollywood sets than real life."

"What about rehearsals?" Howard looked around. "And where will the band stay, as well as the rest of the team?"

"They're not, and before you ask, neither are you. We've been joined at the freaking hip for a decade, and it's time I was out on my own."

"You're firing me?" Howard nearly shouted, and Wilson shook his head.

"No, I'm not firing you. I'm kicking you out of my private life. You've been living in my house, running my career, my personal appearances, everything, for a decade. You will continue to run my career, but that's all. I want my own life, so you'll need to get your own place to live." Wilson had grown to resent his friend and manager's intrusions into his life lately. He knew Howard was looking out for him, but Wilson was a big boy, and he could take care of himself.

Wilson fished the key to the house that the Realtor had given him out of his pocket, unlocked the door, and pushed it open. After stepping inside, he waited for Howard, who followed along behind like a kicked puppy.

"If you're really going to do this, you're going to need me here," Howard said and began looking around, and Wilson could see his manager's mind was already whirling. "We could blow out that back wall and enlarge the place, add a master suite and a great room with a studio off it."

"Howard!" Wilson raised his voice. "You are here for just a few days, and then you're going back to LA. I'm not adding on to the house so you can stay here. I want my own life, Howard. Why is that so hard for you to understand? I want you to do your job and to keep doing it as well as you have been. You're a great manager, but I expect you to listen to me."

"You can't be serious about living... here?" Howard asked him as he stood in the middle of the living room, motioning around him.

"At least it's real here, and it feels right."

"But you're contracted to do that movie in a few months, and they paid you a lot of money already." Howard had snapped back into business mode, which was a relief to see, because it meant he was processing what was happening.

"I'll still do the movie, and then come back here. I plan to live here. This is going to be home. I'm going to put down real roots, far away from groupies and fake parties, where everyone is more concerned about what you're wearing and who you are than the person on the inside." Wilson walked to where Howard stood gaping at him, his boots clicking on the wood floors, the sound echoing off the walls in the empty room. "I need this, and so do you. You've been living for me for so long you don't know how to do anything different. Find yourself someone to love. Settle down and have a house full of kids, if that's what you want. But I've decided what I'm going to do." Damn, that felt good to say.

Howard continued looking around. "While we're here, we may as well look around. And then can we head back to the car and the hotel? I have calls to make." Wilson didn't pay Howard much attention as he looked around the house again. He'd bought it based on website photos and a virtual tour, and the place looked exactly as he expected it to. The house wasn't fancy, but it felt comfortable. "We could bring in a designer to make the place livable," Howard said from across the room, and Wilson ignored him. He wanted to furnish the house the way he wanted it. No designer geegaw, and no fancy crap like the place in LA.

"No thanks," Wilson said with a touch of pleasure. He wanted this to be his place and to feel like him, not someone else. "I'm going to do it myself." Howard laughed, and Wilson turned and glared at him. "You're treading on thin ice, Howard," Wilson said very sternly.

"Come on. I had to do the place in LA for you. It had to fit your image."

Now it was Wilson's turn to scoff. "You mean *your* image. You furnished it the way you wanted it when I was out of town, remember? But that's okay, considering you helped pay for the place." Wilson waited for Howard's brain to process what he'd said.

"No, I didn't. That house was yours… is yours."

"And you think I let you live there all those years for free? Please. My accountant has deducted your rent from your percentage for the last decade, at market rates, I might add. Your percentage did not include free rent." Wilson walked over to

Howard, staring him down. "When we started, you were my best friend, but somewhere along the way, you figured you were entitled. Well, I figured you weren't. You're a good manager, but you turned into a crappy friend who only told me what I wanted to hear. We grew up in Oshkosh, Wisconsin, for Christ's sake, and as soon as I hit it big, you glommed onto all the LA lifestyle my money could afford. I'm tired of it, and I need a rest." If possible, Howard's expression looked like a deflated hot-air balloon.

"Jesus, Willie, I—"

"Don't call me Willie here. It's Wilson or Will, like when we were kids. We had such dreams, and they never looked like that crap in LA, remember? We were going to help our families and make great music. We made the music, but we helped no one but ourselves." Wilson stared into his friend's eyes. "I don't want to do that anymore, and I expect you to listen, or I'll find someone who will. And if I get the slightest hint that you can't be trusted, I'll pull the plug on you so fast it'll make your head spin. Am I making myself clear?"

"You don't trust me?" Howard asked, looking a bit like the kid Wilson had known back in eighth grade, when they'd first met.

"I don't know," Wilson answered honestly. "So if you want me to, you'd better demonstrate it. I'm sorry it has to be this way, but it does. Now, tomorrow I want you to go back to LA, and I want you to arrange for the sale of all the god-awful crap in the Brentwood house. I'll be back in LA in a few days, and we can talk then. I suggest you think about what you really want. We're not kids anymore, and I don't want to live like one."

"I think I understand." Howard looked serious and focused, a look Wilson hadn't seen in a while.

"I hope you do." Wilson walked toward the bedrooms. "And one more thing. You are forbidden from telling anyone where I am under almost any circumstances. I don't want reporters or wannabes beating a path to my door. I want a home. You are welcome here as long as you can be civil and as long as you respect my boundaries." Howard nodded. "You've been good to me, but I've been good to you as well."

"I never knew you felt this way," Howard said with a touch of regret.

"You would have if you'd have listened. I've been saying for months that I haven't been happy and wanted to get out of LA, but you kept passing it off." Wilson knew in his heart that Howard hadn't been malicious. He'd been focused on business and Wilson's career instead of on Wilson himself. "So I'm going to live here, and I'll commute when I need to."

Howard nodded and let out a huge sigh. "I guess I haven't been much of a friend, have I?" Wilson didn't answer. Howard's question was enough for Wilson to know that he'd finally gotten through to him. Wilson finished his walk-through of the house before stepping outside into the late-afternoon sun. "Can we go back to the hotel? I really do need to make those calls, plus a few more now."

"That's fine. You can make your calls, and I'm going to look around town. We can go to dinner at that steak place we passed on the way. I'm in the mood for a good old-fashioned steak dinner, and since this is beef country, I bet it'll be damned good. I'll even let you buy." Howard actually laughed, and Wilson put his arm around his friend's shoulders.

THE RESTAURANT was hopping when they walked in, and the hostess looked frazzled and worn. She must have been running to beat the band all evening. "I'm sorry. It'll be a while," she said. "We just got a large group. Would you mind waiting?" she said as pleasantly as she could.

"No problem, darlin'," Wilson answered in his deep voice, and he saw her eyes widen and then her cheeks flush. Wilson had gotten used to having that effect on women; it was part of how he made his money. "I'm Wilson, and you can call us when our table's ready."

"Of course, sir," she told him, and Wilson saw her look at him like something in the back of her mind said she should know him, but she couldn't quite place him. That was fine. Wilson didn't really want to be recognized or given special treatment. Whenever he was recognized in LA, people fawned all over him, tripping over their own feet to get him whatever he wanted.

"You know, if you'd told her who you were, you wouldn't have to wait," Howard whispered from next to him once they'd sat on one of the benches.

"That's not what I want here, and waiting for a table is fine." Wilson rested back against the wall. He loved watching people, though it was something he rarely got to do. The door opened and a large group of men entered.

"You did make a reservation?" an attractive shorter man asked the tall man behind him.

"Of course, Wally," the tall, broad-shouldered man answered patiently before walking to the hostess. She must have told them it would be a few minutes, because the six of them walked to where he and Howard were sitting, filling the bench across from them. They began to talk animatedly amongst themselves, but Wilson noticed the smaller man, Wally, peering at him every few seconds. Finally, Wally stood up and walked over.

"Excuse me, but you're Willie Meadows, aren't you?" Wally asked in just above a whisper. "I have all your CDs, and we just love your music."

"Thank you," Wilson said. He encountered this all the time, although rarely was he approached so politely.

"Are you waiting for a table?" Wally asked, and Wilson could see the excitement behind Wally's eyes looking like a cherry bomb about ready to burst. "We made reservations for eight, but one couple couldn't make it. You and your friend would be welcome to join us. I promise we won't gush over you... too much. They're busy tonight, so the wait could be awhile."

Wilson's stomach had been grumbling for a while, and he knew Howard was hungry as well. "If you really don't mind, but only if you promise to treat me like everyone else."

"Dakota," Wally said, turning to the other man, "these two gentlemen are joining us. They've already been waiting awhile, and we have extra room." Just like that, Wilson found himself included. He wasn't sure this was a good idea, but Wally seemed nice, and unlike other people who had recognized him, Wally didn't yell out his name or make a scene. It also occurred to Wilson that if he was going to live here, he would need to be a part of the community and make friends.

The hostess approached and led the group back toward a large, round table. "I'm Wilson, and this is Howard," he said, shaking hands all around.

"I'm Wally, and this is Dakota, Phillip, Haven, David, and Mario. It's nice to meet you."

Greetings were exchanged all around the table, and then everyone sat down.

"This is a bit of a celebration," Wally said from across the table. "Dakota just finished his residency, and he's opening a medical practice here in town." Wally looked at Dakota, and Wilson immediately knew they were a couple. It was obvious just by the way they looked at one another. Wilson felt Howard tense slightly next to him, but Wilson ignored it. As he watched the others, Wilson realized they were all couples. Wilson knew he was gay, he'd accepted that some time ago, but for career reasons he'd always been very careful, because fame and success were fleeting. Wilson knew that all it might take was one small thing to end everything he'd worked for. So while he'd spent a lot of time around gay people—he lived in LA, after all—his own sexuality was a closely guarded secret.

Their server approached the table, and everyone placed drink orders. Pretty much everyone ordered a beer, including Wilson, but Howard ordered a martini. Thankfully, no one other than Wally seemed to have recognized him, and Wally hadn't said a word. "So what brings you to our little town?" Dakota asked from next to Wally.

"I just bought a place and I've decided to move here. It's a little north of town."

"That wouldn't be the Henfield place, would it?" Dakota must have seen the surprise on Wilson's face, because he explained, "It's a small town. There may be lots of land, but there's a lot more cattle than people, and everyone tends to know everyone else." Dakota sipped from his beer. "Did you buy the horses as well? Henfield had some amazing animals."

"No. The place is very clean, but all the animals were gone by the time I looked at it. I would have liked to see the place with horses in the paddocks." Wilson could feel a touch of excitement shoot through him as he thought of raising horses on his land.

"Have you decided what you're going to do with the place?" Haven asked.

"Not yet." He really hadn't thought much beyond finding someplace with room to spread out and get away from the city. "I happened to see an ad for the place on a real estate site, and the idea of living here appealed to me. I haven't made many decisions beyond the actual purchase." Wilson hoped he didn't sound like too big a fool. What sort of person buys a small ranch sight unseen with no plans as to what to do with it? Maybe Howard was right and he was being stupid about this whole thing.

"Have you thought of raising horses? That land is perfect for it, but Mrs. Henfield couldn't keep up with everything once her husband died. That's why she sold," Wally explained.

Wilson nodded but didn't commit. Saying anything would mean revealing the fact that he didn't know a thing about horses, or anything else about the country, for that matter. Thankfully, as

Wilson's nerves began to ramp up, their server approached the table and took their orders. Once she left, the conversation veered around to other subjects. Wilson learned that Wally, Dakota, Haven, and Phillip owned quite a large ranch, and that they'd been friends and business partners for a few years now. He also learned that David and Mario worked on the ranch as well.

Howard elbowed him under the table and looked toward the restroom. Wilson knew what that look meant, he'd seen it a number of times before, but for now Wilson chose to ignore it. Whatever was bothering Howard would wait until the ride back to the hotel.

"So what do you do?" Phillip asked, and Wilson heard a *humph* as Wally appeared to elbow him in the side.

"It's all right," Wilson said to Wally, and Phillip glared indignantly at his friend. "I'm a singer," Wilson said in a low voice, and he waited. Wally had already recognized him, and he thought Dakota might have as well.

"Willie Meadows," Wally stage-whispered, and Wilson watched as the others' eyes widened. Wilson got ready to bid a hasty retreat from the table.

"Wally listens to your music all the time," David said. "Nearly drove us crazy when your last CD came out." David's matter-of-fact tone, combined with the no-nonsense looks he was getting from around the table, allowed Wilson to breathe a sigh of relief. "So why are you really here?" David asked.

"I needed time away from the city and everything that goes with it. I bought the ranch because I needed room to breathe without managers and all the hangers-on that come with what I do."

Dakota looked at the others around the table. "If you want peace, that's what you'll get. None of us will mention anything to anyone. Holden Ranch is just a few miles away from your place, and you're welcome there anytime." The food arrived, and once again the conversation continued, and thankfully it didn't center on him. Instead, they talked about cattle, horses, and of all things, the price of feed and hay. For the first time in almost a decade, Wilson felt like a regular person, and damn if that didn't feel good.

Once dinner was over, everyone paid their bills, which was eye-opening for Wilson. He was so used to paying the bill for everyone whenever he went out that he nearly choked when his check came and it was for fifty bucks plus tip. He couldn't remember the last time he'd seen a check that small or had food and company that good. Leaving the restaurant, Wilson shook hands with each of the guys. "It was great to meet all of you," Wilson said, feeling surprisingly comfortable.

"I was serious—if you need anything, just give us a call." Dakota gave Wilson his phone number, shook his hand firmly, and the guys headed toward their trucks as Wilson headed to the rented Lexus.

"I had a great time," Wilson said once he was belted into the passenger seat next to Howard.

"Those people were just interested in you because of who you are," Howard cautioned. In LA, most people had to get to him through Howard. He was used to playing Willie Meadows's gatekeeper, and he took that duty rather seriously.

"I don't think so. Most of them had no idea who I was, and once they knew, they didn't really care." Wilson smiled at the thought that he might be able to actually have friends—real friends. He shifted on the seat so he could look at Howard. "Do you have any idea how long it's been since I had friends of any kind?" A wave of sadness hit Wilson in the gut like a punch.

"I know, and I don't blame you," Howard said as he started the car. "But what you have comes with a price. You know that and you have to be careful. Remember Calvin?"

Wilson shuddered and tried to put the humiliation out of his mind. "I know," Wilson said quietly. He knew that very well.

"I'm also worried about you hanging around with them. This may be a small town in the middle of nowhere, but it's a small world, and your career hung by a thread for a while. It's been forgotten now and you want it to remain that way, especially out here." Howard's voice held an edge, and Wilson knew exactly what he was talking about.

They pulled into the hotel, and Wilson got out of the car, heading straight to his room. Once the door was closed and he knew no one could see him, he opened his bag and pulled out the whiskey bottle that he seemed to keep perpetually close at hand. He opened the bottle, poured some into one of those disposable hotel cups that came wrapped in plastic, and downed it in a gulp. The warmth, as false and fake as the clothes he wore, slipped down his throat before settling in his stomach. He knew this wouldn't do him any good, and it never made the loneliness go away for long. He thought about having more, but closed the bottle and stared at it for a while before opening it again and pouring the liquor in the sink. It was time to make some changes. Throwing away the cup, he was about to get ready for bed when a knock on the door was quickly followed by Howard walking into the room, his phone at his ear. It was going to be another long, lonely night. Wilson reminded himself not to give Howard a key to his room.

WILSON KNEW that Howard would sleep for hours in the morning, so he got up, showered, and dressed. After leaving his manager a note, he took the car and drove back out to his house. He really wanted to be able to take a good look around without Howard explaining what was wrong with everything. When he turned into the drive, Wilson was surprised to see an old truck pulled off into the yard near the barn. And when he parked the car, Wilson saw someone come out of the barn.

"Morning, mister," the man said, and as he walked toward the car, Wilson saw he couldn't have been much more than twenty, skinny as a beanpole, but with an earnest expression that Wilson found endearing. "Do you know what happened?" he asked, motioning around him. "I was supposed to come here for a job, but everything's gone." He looked almost brokenhearted.

"I'm the new owner," Wilson explained through the open car window.

"What happened to Mrs. Henfield?" the kid asked, and he started to shake a little. "She wrote me some months back, offering me a job training her horses. I got hurt and told her I needed to heal up, so she told me to come when I was better." Dang, if he'd been sick, he certainly didn't look like he'd had time to heal. His face was slightly drawn and thin. Wilson also couldn't help noticing that the end of his belt hung a little long, like he was notching it in a lot more than he used to.

"I'm sorry, but her husband died, and she sold the ranch," Wilson explained.

The kid definitely looked heartbroken, and he turned around and walked back toward his old truck. Wilson watched as he opened the door and climbed inside but made no move to start the engine. Instead, Wilson saw him lean his head against the steering wheel like he didn't quite know what to do. Wilson pulled the car to what looked like a decent place to park and got out, wandering over to the kid's truck. The young man hadn't moved, and if Wilson hadn't known better, he'd almost think the kid was asleep, except when he looked through the window, Wilson saw him shaking.

Wilson tapped lightly on the window, and the kid lifted his head. The fear Wilson saw in those deep brown eyes shocked him. "What's going on?"

"Nothing. I just needed this job real bad, and now it's gone. I ain't got the money to fill up the tank to get somewhere else, let alone eat. But that ain't yer problem." The kid wiped his face and started the engine.

Wilson stepped back as the kid put the truck in gear and started down the driveway. Wilson listened to the truck as it turned onto the road and sped up before sputtering a few times. Wilson saw the kid maneuver the truck off the road before it died. He sighed and walked back to his car. After starting the engine, he drove down the driveway and stopped behind where the kid's truck had run out of gas. Wilson got out and walked up to the driver's door. He saw the kid once again slumped over the steering wheel, and this time, Wilson pulled the door open. The screech of metal was almost deafening, and he realized the truck was barely holding itself together. "Come on. I'm heading back to town, and I can take you with me." There was no way Wilson could leave him out here. When he didn't move, Wilson held out his hand. "It's okay."

"No, it's not," the kid said as he got out of the truck. He looked sort of glassy-eyed, and Wilson was beginning to wonder when he'd last eaten, or slept, for that matter.

"Go get in the car," Wilson said as he wrenched the truck door closed. He watched as the kid walked alongside the truck reaching into the back for what looked like some sort of old duffel bag. He lifted it out and nearly fell over as he did. Wilson popped open the trunk, and the kid set his duffel inside.

"I'm real sorry about this, mister," he said, looking toward the ground.

"Don't think twice about it," Wilson said. He understood where the kid was coming from. No, he hadn't been out stranded in the middle of nowhere alone. Instead, he'd been stranded in LA, which was probably worse in a lot of ways. "The name's Wilson, by the way," he said with a smile he hoped looked reassuring.

"Steve," the kid said, and after lightly closing the trunk, he slid into the passenger seat and closed the door, keeping as far away from Wilson as he could.

"I won't hurt you, I promise." The haunted look in the kid's eyes told him that wasn't going to soothe him any. Something pretty bad had happened to this kid, and he was mighty scared and nervous. Wilson put the car in gear and pulled onto the road, heading back toward town. When he pulled into the hotel parking lot, Steve got really nervous, and at first Wilson thought he was going to jump out of the car. "This is where I'm staying. I need to make sure my friend is up, and then we can get something to eat."

Wilson got out of the car, taking the keys with him, just because it was prudent, and knocked on Howard's door.

"I was wondering where you went. I'm starving," Howard said as he closed his door and walked toward the car. He stopped when he saw the front seat was already occupied. "What's this?" he asked, glaring quizzically at Wilson. "You picked up some kid?" Howard hissed.

"That's enough," Wilson snapped, his teeth clenched. "Remember our conversation yesterday. You work for me, not the other way around. I do not need to justify myself to you." Wilson stared at Howard to make sure he got the message.

What he saw in return was hurt and concern. "You picked up some kid?" Howard asked again. "What were you thinking? He could have robbed you or worse."

Wilson chuckled slightly as he looked to where Steve sat in the car. "He probably hasn't eaten in a while, and I don't think he's feeling well. Mrs. Henfield offered him a job sometime back, and he showed up today only to find the place empty." Howard looked skeptical. "His old truck ran out of gas at the end of the drive, and he doesn't have money to go anywhere else. I couldn't leave him there." Wilson looked at the car once again, surprised at how his eyes were drawn to the man sitting in the passenger seat. The kid really wasn't much to look at, well, maybe not compared to the golden boys he'd seen in California, but Steve was real. Wilson shook his head slightly, pushing those thought from his brain. Steve was someone who needed help, nothing more. He would make sure Steve was okay and send him on his way. "Let's go get something to eat. Steve can come with us, and then we'll figure out how to get his truck brought into town. Then you can head back to LA to get things moving. I'll be along in a few days to make final arrangements."

Howard looked skeptical, and Wilson would have said more, but Steve opened the car door and climbed out. Closing it, he stood by the car, looking like he would fall over at any moment. Wilson glanced at Howard and saw the minute the fight went out of him.

"We're going to get something to eat," Wilson said, and Steve nodded.

"I'll get my things out of the trunk," Steve said, taking a few steps toward the back of the car before his legs seemed to buckle. He steadied himself, and Wilson moved toward him without another thought.

"Steady. You're okay." He took Steve's arm to keep him from falling. "I meant for you to come with us. You need to eat, and we can figure out what to do afterwards. Okay?" Wilson said, and Steve turned his face to him, big eyes meeting his in an expression of such relieved gratitude that Wilson couldn't help smiling. "Come on, we'll get your bag once we've eaten." Wilson could see a touch of reticence in Steve, but he suspected that his hunger probably got the best of him because Wilson saw Steve steady himself. When he got back into the car, Howard flashed a put-out look toward the front seat before climbing in the back and closing his door. Wilson hurried around to the driver's seat and drove down the street to a diner he'd seen the night before.

Wilson kept an eye on Steve as they walked into the crowded, noisy restaurant. Servers hurried from table to table, orders were called noisily back to the kitchen, and the entire place smelled like it had been serving fried food for the last fifty years. "Table for three," Wilson said when someone stopped, and she motioned toward a table in the front.

"Someone will be right with you," she said before grabbing a pot of coffee from a nearby station and hurrying away. They made their way to the table. Wilson slipped into the booth and Howard sat on the other side. Steve looked at both of them and then sat next to Wilson before looking at him quizzically.

"Order whatever you want," Wilson told him, and Steve opened the menu. Wilson did the same, and when the server came, he placed an order for some fruit and toast. Howard ordered a huge breakfast, and Wilson saw Steve look at him, silently questioning, before ordering the largest breakfast on the menu, with a side of pancakes. That confirmed Wilson's suspicions that Steve hadn't eaten in a while, and when the food came, Steve set to it, eating as though it might be his last meal.

"So, Steve, what do you plan to do now?" Howard asked, and Wilson flashed him a look that Howard ignored.

"I don't know," Steve answered around the food he was eating as fast as he could. "I train horses. That's what Mrs. Henfield hired me to do, and I was really counting on that job." The sadness and desperation in Steve's eyes cut to Wilson's heart. Mrs. Henfield probably had offered Steve a job, and while it wasn't Wilson's fault that she couldn't make good on the promise, he still felt a touch guilty because he'd bought the ranch. Steve went back to eating, his eyes never straying from his plate.

"What are you going to do with the ranch? Are you going to raise horses? Because I could help you...," Steve offered.

"He's just going to live on the ranch," Howard explained before Wilson could answer. "I doubt very much if Willie... Wilson is going to actually raise horses there."

"I haven't decided what I'm going to do yet," Wilson corrected, a little more loudly and forcefully than he intended, but it had the desired effect, and Howard remained quiet for the rest of breakfast. Wilson didn't know what had come over his friend, but he wasn't too happy with his behavior. They ate quietly from then on, with Howard and him occasionally exchanging looks. Steve seemed oblivious and just continued eating. The few times he looked up, Wilson saw that same worried look he had earlier.

Once they were done, Wilson paid the check, and they headed out and back to the car. They stopped at a gas station, and after borrowing a gas can (and filling it up), they drove back out to the ranch.

Wilson poured the gas into Steve's truck, and it started. "This should get you back to town," Wilson said.

"Thank you," Steve told him, and after getting his duffel bag out of the trunk, he placed it in the back of the truck. Wilson watched as Steve got in the truck and drove away.

"Can we get going now? I need to get back to LA." Howard seemed to be getting squirrely, so Wilson agreed, and after taking a long look at what would be his new home, Wilson pointed the car back toward town.

Chapter Two

STEVE DIDN'T drive far—he knew he couldn't, and he had no place to go. If he went back to town, he'd have no place to stay, and there would be no one to help him. He was on his own, and he needed a place to stay. Wilson had been nice to him, and he was grateful, he really was, but Steve was desperate and he didn't have any other place to go right now. So he pulled off the road and waited until Wilson's car passed. He'd heard them talking at the diner, and he knew Wilson was going to go to LA, so once they'd passed, he drove back to the farm and parked on the far side of the barn so no one would see his truck. Walking around, Steve pulled out his duffel bag and carried it into the barn. He wasn't about to break into Wilson's house, but he hoped Wilson wouldn't mind too much if he stayed in the barn for a few days.

He'd eaten, but now he was tired and needed a place to sleep and get some of his strength back. He'd left in a hurry, wanting to get here to start his job. Too bad that was gone, too, along with everything else in his life. Steve felt almost like his life was over, but even those thoughts were overridden by the need for sleep.

When he'd been here earlier, he'd seen that the stalls were all clean and empty, as was most of the rest of the barn, but in one of the small rooms, he found a couple of old saddle blankets. He laid them out on the floor of one of the stalls to provide some padding on the concrete. Steve unrolled the blankets he'd been using when he'd slept in the back of the truck, and using some of his clothes as a pillow, he laid down on his makeshift bed and closed his eyes. His body was so weary that Steve fell asleep almost instantly. He slept deeply and didn't move until he felt someone shaking his shoulder. The hand felt warm and… wait, something inside Steve's mind wondered what was happening, and he forced his eyes open.

"What are you doing here?"

Steve lifted his head and found himself looking at Wilson. "I…," Steve started to answer, but he couldn't. Everything that had happened to him came bubbling to the surface all at once, and Steve put his face in the clothes he'd been using as a pillow. He tried to stop the tears, but they came unbidden.

"Hey, it's okay," Wilson said soothingly, but Steve barely heard him. He felt Wilson's hand on his back and flinched slightly, moving away as he tried to get ahold of himself.

"I didn't have a place to go," Steve answered when he could get his voice to work. "I'm sorry." He stood up and began gathering his things. "I thought you were leaving." Steve needed to get out of here as quickly as he could before Wilson got angry with him. Not that he could blame him at all. Wilson had every right to be mad at him, and he could call the police. Steve sort of hoped he did; at least in jail he'd get fed and have a place to sleep. He actually felt more tears run down his cheeks when he thought of just how desperate he was.

"Howard was going back. I'm staying for a few days to get things in order here." Wilson actually smiled, and Steve braced to be hit the way his father had always hit him. "I'm not going to hurt you, but I think you owe me some sort of explanation. I helped you out, and you snuck back onto my property. What were you going to do, live in my barn?"

"Yes," Steve answered truthfully. "I had no place to go, and it was warm and dry here." It wasn't as though he was going to get very far in the truck with only the gas Wilson had given him and no money to buy more.

"What were you going to do for food?" Wilson asked, and Steve shrugged. He really hadn't gotten much further than a roof over his head. "Come on," Wilson said, and Steve gathered his things and followed Wilson outside. A shiny new truck was parked in front of the house, and Steve looked at it strangely.

"Where's the car?" Steve inquired and held tighter to his bag when Wilson tried to take it from him.

"That was a rental. Howard returned it to the airport, and I figured I'd need a truck around here, so I bought one." Steve couldn't help whistling. Wilson must be rich if he could afford to just buy a truck like that. "I said I wasn't going to hurt you, and I meant it." Steve saw that Wilson had his hand out, so he handed him the duffel, and Wilson put it in the back of the truck. "Get in. I'm taking you back to town."

Steve didn't see where he had any alternative, so he got inside and pulled on the seat belt before crossing his arms over his chest, sinking back into himself where he couldn't be hurt. He heard the other door open and close, then the engine started, and Steve watched as they pulled away from the ranch.

The scenery passed by them, and Steve sat quietly, afraid to move or ask any questions. He fully expected to be dropped off at the sheriff's office.

Steve was so nervous he could barely stand it. He had no idea what was going to happen to him. When Wilson drove through town, Steve watched each building as it passed. He had no idea where the sheriff's office was, but they had to be getting close now. Steve felt the truck turn and looked out the front window. The building looked familiar, and Steve realized Wilson had brought him to his hotel. Steve looked across the bench seat and knew he should have known. Wilson parked and got out of the truck. Steve did the same, figuring he might as well get this over with. Grabbing his bag, he followed Wilson up to the entrance and through the hallway to the room that Wilson unlocked.

Steve walked inside and saw the single huge bed in the bright room. Wilson was already pulling the curtains, and Steve let his bag drop to the floor. He figured he might as well do what he had to. God knows he'd done what he needed to survive before. Pulling off his shirt, Steve reached for his pants as he saw Wilson turn around.

"What are you doing?" Wilson asked loudly, and Steve wanted to hide.

"I thought you…," Steve stammered, and he clamped his eyes closed. He was so stupid. Steve immediately tried to cover himself and bent over to grab his shirt.

"What I want is for you to talk to me for a few minutes, and then you can get in bed and rest. You're obviously exhausted, and judging from breakfast, I'm assuming you haven't been eating regularly." Wilson sat on the far edge of the bed, looking at him over his shoulder as Steve put his shirt back on.

"Do you want to tell me what happened to you?" Wilson asked, and Steve shook his head. "Is the law after you?"

"No," Steve answered softly. "I'm not a fugitive." At least he was grateful for that. Steve hoped that Wilson wouldn't press him about his past because that was just too hard for him to talk about right now. Maybe he could eventually, but not right now. The pain and hurt were too close to the surface, and if he tried to put them into words, he'd never be able to control himself. Besides, Wilson was almost a total stranger, and he wasn't about to unload all his baggage on him.

"Will you tell me your last name?" Wilson asked with a half smile.

"Peterson," Steve answered truthfully. Wilson deserved to know that much. He'd been good to him so far, but Steve kept wondering how long it would last.

"Look, Steve, your past is your business, and I won't pry," Wilson said soothingly, and Steve breathed a small sigh, his relief coming on so many levels. "Rest if you want. No one is going to hurt you or take advantage of you." Wilson's eyes hardened, and for some strange reason that comforted Steve. Wilson got up and pulled back the covers on the bed. The clean sheets and soft covers called to Steve like a siren song. He wasn't sure how long he'd slept in the barn, but his body was screaming for rest. Taking off his shoes, he lay down, and Wilson turned off the lights except for a small one near the chair. Steve closed his eyes, the bedding and soft pillows surrounding him, and he felt reasonably safe.

Wilson moved around for a few seconds, and after that, all Steve heard was the occasional rustle of a page being turned in a book and the soft hum of the air conditioner. Steve felt safe, and when he cracked his eyes open, he saw Wilson looking at him with a slight smile before going back to his book. When Steve closed his eyes again, he could see that smile in his mind's eyes like a picture, and this time his eyes stayed closed and Steve fell asleep.

When he woke later, the room was dark and he was alone. Sitting up, Steve looked around the room, but the only evidence he saw of Wilson was his suitcase sitting neatly on the bench and his book folded over the arm of the chair. All the lights were off, but there was still sunlight peeking around the edge of the curtains, so he hadn't slept the entire day away. He pushed back the covers and stretched before getting out of the bed and carefully standing up. He felt better than he had in a long time. Looking around for a piece of paper, Steve turned on a light. When he found a pad and pen in one of the drawers, he sat at the desk and began to compose a note to Wilson. He got it half-written before the door opened.

Wilson strode into the room carrying two bags of food, a bottle tucked up under his arm. "I hope you're feeling better."

"I am, thank you," Steve answered as he looked down at the note he'd been writing. Wilson walked to the desk and set down the things he was carrying. Steve tried to rip the note off the pad and hide it, but he wasn't in time.

"You were going to leave?" Wilson asked, setting the note back down on the desk.

Steve nodded slowly. "You've been so nice, I figured you'd want me out of your hair. I appreciate what you've done to help me. It's more than most people would do, and I'm really grateful, but you don't want me hanging around." Steve saw Wilson stare at him hard and long. The intensity of Wilson's gaze made him uncomfortable, because he knew what that meant—it was time for him to pay for Wilson's kindness.

"Why don't you let me worry about what I want," Wilson said with raised eyebrows. He reached to the desk and handed Steve one of the bags. "I wasn't sure what you'd like, so I got you a hamburger and a chicken sandwich." Wilson moved the things to the side of the desk and sat in the chair before opening his bag and laying out the food.

Steve approached, wondering just what was going on. Wilson was being so nice to him, and every time Steve thought he knew what the other man wanted, he was surprised. He stood looking at Wilson, trying to figure him out what was happening.

"Pull up the other chair," Wilson told him after swallowing a french fry. "I think you have the wrong idea, and we need to get something straight." The touch of hardness in Wilson's voice made Steve pause, but he pulled up the chair and sat across from Wilson. "Your past is your own, and I won't pry into it. If you say no one is after you and you haven't done anything wrong, then I believe you, and you needn't tell me anything else unless you want to. But we need to get something clear. I'm trying to help you, and I don't expect anything in return, at least not what you seem to think I want in return." Wilson's expression softened, and when he smiled, Steve saw the warmest, handsomest man he'd ever seen in his life. Sure, he wasn't interested in sleeping with someone because he had to, but part of him sort of wished Wilson had taken him up on his implied offer. Wilson seemed kind, and it had been a long time since anyone had shown him any kindness.

"I understand, and I'm sorry." Steve opened the bag and pulled out a sandwich wrapped in paper. He didn't care what it was; he was so hungry he was tempted to eat the paper along with the rest of it.

"Don't be. You've had a tough time of it, that's obvious." Wilson continued eating, and Steve saw Wilson watching him closely. When Wilson turned him down, at first Steve thought that maybe he wasn't gay, but straight men didn't look at other guys the way Wilson was looking at him, at least he didn't think so. "I do want to make you an offer, though. I have the ranch, and while I'm not sure what I'm going to do with it yet, I'm going to need someone to take care of it for me, so I was wondering if you'd like the job. I know you said you train horses, and I don't have any now, but when I get back maybe we can look into getting some."

Steve set down his sandwich. He knew he was gawking, but he couldn't believe his ears. "You're offering me a job after what I did?"

"What did you do? You slept in my barn because you didn't have another place to go. That's hardly the worst thing someone has tried to do to me. Mrs. Henfield offered you a job, and she knew her stuff, so if you're willing, I'll hire you on to take care of the place until I figure out what I'm going to do. Then you can decide if you want to stay on or not."

Steve continued staring. He could hardly believe his luck. "You're serious? You're giving me a job?" Steve swallowed around the huge lump in his throat and looked away. He didn't want Wilson to see him cry. That had already happened once, in a moment of weakness, and he wasn't going to let it happen again. "And you don't want anything from me?"

"Except a fair day's work," Wilson clarified, and Steve thought he was going to say something else. There was a strange look in his eye, like he wanted to say something, but part of him wouldn't allow it, like Wilson was warring with himself. "We'll agree on a weekly wage, and since I have to go back to California in a few days, we'll make up a room in the house for you to stay in. And we'll make sure you have food and everything you need. When I get back, we'll make a plan as to what we're going to do."

While Wilson was talking, Steve had practically inhaled his food. He knew his mama would have been appalled, she was always one for proper manners, but he was so hungry he couldn't stop himself. "You want me to help you decide what to do with the ranch? You bought it and you don't know what you're gonna do with it?" Steve asked. "It's perfect for raising and training horses. There's already a ring and plenty of almost new stalls in the barn. Even the pastures and paddocks are perfect for horses." Steve stopped himself from running on. It wasn't polite. If Wilson wanted to do something else with his land, that was up to him. Steve would do his best to take care of it for him, that was for certain.

Wilson actually laughed. "I suppose it is. I met some people in town the other day, and they have a ranch not far from mine. I was thinking we could stop by their place. They know this area, and it will give you someone to call if you have a problem while I'm gone."

Steve nodded and continued eating. It sounded like Wilson had thought of almost everything, and Steve smiled at his benefactor. He couldn't believe his luck, or that Wilson was being so good to someone he'd barely even met. Steve always believed there were kind people in this world, but it just seemed that lately he hadn't had the good fortune to meet any of them. Maybe his luck was finally starting to change. He wanted to believe it so badly. "For now you just want me to take care of the house and barn until you get back?" Steve wanted to make sure he had it right.

"That and sort of watch over the place. I shouldn't be gone too long," Wilson said, and Steve nodded once, relieved that he had a job and even a place to live, at least until Wilson found out what he'd done. Then maybe he wouldn't have that. He hadn't lied when he'd said he wasn't on the run from the law, but he hadn't exactly been forthcoming, either. "Finish up your dinner, and we'll get going."

Steve was nearly done, and he finished the last of the food, feeling more alive after the deep sleep and with a full belly, which he hadn't had in a while. Once he was done, Steve cleaned up the papers and threw them in the trash with Wilson's. Wilson picked up Steve's bag and handed it to him. Then Steve followed him out of the room. Wilson closed the door behind them, and they walked through the hotel and out to Wilson's truck.

THE FIRST stop was an old hardware store, where Wilson bought some basic kitchen supplies. Well, actually, Steve picked stuff out. It was funny—Wilson didn't seem to know what he was doing, and every time Steve picked something up, Wilson just placed it on their pile of stuff. What clued him in was when Steve picked up a fancy espresso maker and Wilson added that too. Steve made sure to put it back. Once they had paid for the kitchen and bath stuff, they found a five-and-dime, and Wilson bought sheets and some thick pads for sleeping on. "I know it isn't a mattress, but it should be more comfortable than the stall floor until I get back and can arrange for real furniture," Wilson told him, and Steve smiled. They looked mighty comfortable to him, and Wilson had bought two, just to be sure.

"Thank you," Steve said with a smile. He really didn't care about that—he had a job and a place to sleep. Their last stop was a grocery store, and Wilson bought enough food for an army. Once they were done, the bed of the truck was dang near full, and they drove out to the ranch.

Wilson unlocked the door and showed Steve inside. When they got to the kitchen, Steve saw that the refrigerator door was open. He fished around until he got it plugged in, and the motor began to hum. Then he began hauling in the food, putting it and the other things away. While he was working, he thought of his mama and how she always liked things just so. It took him a while before he realized that he'd placed everything like his mama had done in her kitchen, utensils to the right of the stove, then the flatware, with pots and pans in the cupboard below. He missed her so much. She was all he missed from back home, but every time he thought about her, his heart ached.

Wilson's heavy footsteps brought him back to the present. "I put the new stuff in one of the bedrooms. I know it isn't much, and I wish there was time to get everything, but this should hold you until I get back."

Steve closed the cupboard door and turned toward Wilson's deep voice. Their eyes met, and maybe it was the fact that Wilson was being so kind to him, but in that second, Steve thought he saw something that touched his heart. Wilson was truly kind, and when he didn't look away, Steve licked his lips a little and his heart began to speed up. Slowly, he stood up, and Wilson didn't move. "Thank you for everything," Steve said softly, like he was caught in a trance. Wilson's blue eyes looked as deep as any lake he'd ever seen, and Wilson's lips were perfect for kissing. Steve took a small step forward, and Wilson didn't back away. Steve wanted Wilson's arms around him, holding him, keeping him safe.

The pots shifted in the cupboard, and that broke the spell. Wilson looked away, and Steve did the same, feeling a bit foolish. Wilson had already told him he wasn't interested in him like that, and besides, he was just feeling all mushy about his mama and was probably seeing things. Although his entire body usually didn't react when he was just "seeing things."

"Let's get the rest of the stuff inside." Wilson sounded the same as ever, and Steve hurried out to the truck. The only thing in the back was his duffel. As he grabbed it, he saw a truck moving down the road, and he followed it with his eyes as it slowly turned and pulled into the driveway. Steve climbed into the cab of Wilson's truck and crouched low, cracking the other door in case he needed to get out of that side. His heart raced a million miles an hour, and there was no doubt what was causing it this time.

"Wally, Dakota," he heard Wilson call from the house. "What brings you here?" There was a definite smile in Wilson's voice, and Steve made like he was looking for something before getting out of the truck. If Wilson saw his strange behavior, he didn't say anything as he walked to where the others were talking. "Steve, this is Wally and Dakota, they live a few miles away. Guys, this is Steve Peterson. Mrs. Henfield hired him a while ago, and he's going to be looking after the place for me."

"Pleased to meet you, Steve," Wally said, extending his hand. Steve shook hands with Wally and then Dakota, looking first at one then the other. "Is something wrong?" Wally asked, and Steve saw Dakota touch Wally's back slightly. Steve smiled and shook his head.

"Not at all." He could hardly believe it. Wally and Dakota were a couple. They were like him, and they didn't seem to be hiding who they were. Steve looked toward the road and realized he was almost expecting people to come running with pitchforks or something. "Wilson said you lived pretty close."

"Just a few miles away, actually," Dakota said. "We were on our way by and saw your truck. We thought we'd stop to see if you needed anything." Dakota had a great smile, and he was quite handsome. Steve could definitely see what Wally saw in him, but neither of them held a candle to Wilson. Steve's gaze traveled to Wilson, and he smiled before he could stop himself. Then he looked away, realizing how inappropriate he was being.

"Steve is going to be here while I'm gone," Wilson explained.

"If you need anything, come see us. We're a few miles to the west," Dakota said, and then he explained how to get to their place. "Drop in anytime. You'll probably need tools, and we can loan you most of what you need."

"Thank you," Steve said with a smile. "I'll do that."

Everyone began staring like they'd run out of things to say. Wally and Dakota eventually said their goodbyes, and after another round of shaking hands, they got in their truck and drove off, leaving him alone with Wilson once again.

Steve took his things into the house and placed them on the floor of the bedroom Wilson had said he could use.

"I'm going to go back to the hotel, and I'll probably see if I can catch a flight in the next day or so. Do you have a phone?" Wilson asked, and Steve shook his head. "I'll see if I can get the one in the house turned on." Wilson patted his pockets and came up with some sort of card. "Here's my number. You call me if you need something or run into trouble." Wilson handed it to him, and Steve turned it over, peering at the side Wilson hadn't written on.

"Is this you?" Steve read the name and looked up at Wilson, his eyes widening. "You're Willie Meadows."

"Shit," Wilson said under his breath. "All right, yes. I'm Willie Meadows, but I don't want you to tell anyone, because out here I'm just plain Wilson Edwards. I'm trusting you with my secret. If everyone knew, then I wouldn't get any peace, and there would be reporters camped out on the street. I'd never get any quiet."

"I won't tell anyone," Steve said quietly, looking once again at the phone number. He actually had Willie Meadows's phone number.

Wilson scoffed, and Steve looked up from the card. "It's not a holy relic, Steve, it's just a business card, and I'm just another person like you. That's why I didn't tell you before. When people meet Willie, they go all gooey and starry-eyed." Wilson turned and walked toward the door. Steve followed, still holding the card. "Back in LA, everyone treats me like I'm some sort of fucking genius. 'Yes, Willie. You're right, Willie.'" His voice went higher, and Steve chuckled under his breath.

"How about 'You're full of shit, Willie,'" Steve said, and Wilson whirled around. "You have a great life, and you're complaining because your success comes with a price." Steve took a deep breath, but it didn't help. "Try being scared, hungry, and not having any place to sleep except the back of your truck or a stall in someone's barn!" Steve really didn't know where all this was coming from, but once he started he couldn't stop. "So, you're Willie Meadows. Big deal. What you do makes people happy, and if doing what you love comes with a price, then you pay it." Steve saw the anger in Wilson's eyes, and he took a step back, fully expecting to be told to get off Wilson's land.

"Okay," Wilson said. "You made your point." Then he smiled. "I guess I don't have to worry about you just telling me what I want to hear, do I?"

"Nope," Steve answered, feeling relieved shooting off his mouth hadn't gotten him fired and kicked off the ranch after only having a job for a few hours.

"Okay, then. I have your word you'll keep quiet?" Wilson asked, and Steve reassured him his secret was safe. Steve slipped the card in his pocket and made sure his things were all there before following Wilson through the house and out to the truck. "I'll see you in a few days." Wilson reached into his pocket, pulled out some money, and handed it to Steve. "This way you'll be able to fill your tank and get anything you need."

Steve took the money, and Wilson got into the truck. Steve watched as it bounced down the drive before turning onto the road. Steve looked down the road until Wilson disappeared, wondering at his fabulous good luck.

Once Wilson was gone, Steve went back in the house and closed the door. The sun was setting and the light inside was becoming red and pink. After going back to his room, Steve turned on the overhead light and began making up his bed. When he was done, he left the room, turning off the light. Other than the few things in his room, the house was totally empty, and every footstep echoed in the empty rooms. Steve found the door to the basement and turned on the lights. Descending slowly, he looked around and was surprised to find some old wooden chairs sitting in one of the corners. Steve checked them out and found them surprisingly solid, so he figured he'd carry them upstairs and put them on the porch. Grabbing one, he carefully brought it up the stairs.

As he approached the front door, Steve saw a truck pull into the drive. Setting down the chair, Steve crouched down and peered around the edge of the window. The truck stopped about halfway down the drive. The only light inside came from the open basement door, and Steve crawled to the door, and switched off the light. He hoped there were no visible basement windows, but it was too late now. Crawling back to the window, he saw a man get out of the truck and look around the nearly dark yard. Steve knew if they saw his truck behind the barn, he was sunk.

Steve saw a second man get out of the truck, and this one he thought he recognized, but he couldn't be sure. He was afraid to move or make a sound in case they heard him. Curled on the floor, Steve kept his head down and was more than thankful as the last of the sun's light slipped from the sky. The house was completely dark, the only light coming from a pole light out on the far side of the barn. Steve heard footsteps on the porch. Plastering himself against the wall, he could actually see a shadow in the window above him. Steve held his breath and waited, feeling the cold wall against his back.

But now it was concrete, a small enclosure where his dad had put him after a fit of rage. Steve shivered in his shorts and thin T-shirt, the rough concrete hurting his skin with every movement. Pitch blackness surrounded him, and everything smelled dank and old. Where he was, he had no idea. He'd never been here before, probably because he'd never angered his father like this before. Slowly, Steve tried to sit up, and at least he didn't hit his head on anything. Pulling his knees close, he wrapped his arms around them and shook uncontrollably.

The waiting was the hardest part, and Steve knew he was alone and no one would dare come for him. Sounds from outside sometimes made their way to him, but they were faint, and Steve could only catch snippets of anything over the sound of his chattering teeth. His own father had done this to him, the man he thought loved him. Steve thought his heart would break, and after a while he began to wish he were dead.

The shadow moved on, and he heard the footsteps recede. Then everything got quiet. Carefully he moved back into the room, staying on the floor. Headlights turned on, shining into the window, and Steve sank back down, listening as the sound of the engine got softer. Steve lay where he was, breathing through his mouth as he willed his heart to slow down. He had no idea they'd be able to find him so fast. But at least the place had looked empty, and hopefully they'd return home or look for him someplace else.

Standing up, Steve checked one more time that they were truly gone before walking into the kitchen. Opening the refrigerator, Steve had never been so thankful for beer in his life. After cracking one open, he chugged it down and reached for another before stopping himself. Wilson had only bought one case, and Steve didn't need to drink them all at once. Besides, he needed to keep his wits about him. Instead, he had a snack and decided to go to bed.

After eating, Steve silently walked down the hallway to his bedroom. He knew he was being ridiculous, and that they were gone, but part of him was still afraid to make any noise. In the bathroom, he was glad to find hot water, so he immediately grabbed some of the towels Wilson had bought for him and stripped down, taking a quick shower in near total darkness before drying himself and brushing his teeth. Wilson had indeed been good to him, making sure he had everything he would need. With a towel around his waist, Steve walked into the bedroom and pulled on a pair of boxers and a T-shirt before climbing into his makeshift bed. He closed his eyes and tried not to think of the men looking for him. Instead, he found images of Wilson flashing through his mind. He really wished Wilson was here with him. Hell, what he really wished was that Wilson was in the bed with him, holding him in those strong arms and telling him in that deep, rich voice that had charmed millions that everything was going to be okay. He knew he shouldn't be having these kinds of thoughts about his boss, but he couldn't help it. Something in Wilson's kindness touched him. He might never have the actual Wilson hold him in the darkness, but at least he could dream about it.

Chapter Three

"YOU WHAT?" Howard asked, his voice reverberating through the large living room. "You left that... kid at your ranch? Jesus, what will you find when you get back? A hole in the ground where the house once stood?" Howard was pacing the floor, walking back and forth and driving Wilson crazy.

"He's not going to do anything. He's taking care of the ranch, and when I get back he's going to help run the place. Not that any of this is any of your business," Wilson growled at his manager.

"You know he's only glommed onto you because of who you are," Howard warned. "You need to be careful. You know people will try to take advantage of you." Wilson knew Howard was concerned about him, and that was the only reason he didn't take his head off right then and there.

"Calm down. Wally and Dakota will stop by every now and then. Everything is fine. I'm not helpless and I don't appreciate being expected to live my life in the 'World According to Howard'." Wilson locked his eyes onto his manager's, and he saw Howard back down. "Now, how are the arrangements for the disposition of all this crap coming along?" God, he hated this house. Howard had decorated it the way he thought would fit Wilson's image, and at the time it seemed like a good idea, but now, after seeing a little of how things were done in the real West, this stuff was just tacky. The stuffed heads of dead animals on the wall were what disturbed him most. He hated those things. The living room actually had a buffalo head on the wall, and Howard liked to tell people that Willie shot it. Now, Wilson couldn't shoot a gun if his life depended on it. There were elk and deer as well, and a bearskin rug with the head still on it in front of the fake fireplace.

"I wasn't sure what you'd want to take with you," Howard explained as he looked around the room.

"Nothing in this god-awful room. I'm having my bedroom furniture shipped as well as some of the furniture in the other rooms, including yours, so you need to be out tomorrow, because the movers are arriving to pack. The rest is being sold." Wilson wasn't going to sit on this. He wanted all this done so he could get on with his life.

"You can't sell my stuff," Howard protested weakly. He knew as well as Wilson did that Wilson had paid for everything in the house.

"Then you can buy it. But you need to get it out of the house and do it now," Wilson pronounced. "And just for the record, I heard you going on about a party tonight. If you were planning on having it here, you need to cancel it now. No more parties, and no more hangers-on. I'm through with all of it."

"We need to have a farewell party," Howard said.

"No, you need to get your act together and do your job. How is that record deal coming along?" Howard had been working on the deal for his next album for a month, and it wasn't going anywhere.

"They want new material," Howard explained as he flopped onto the saddle-leather sofa—the only piece of furniture in the room that wasn't hideous.

"Fine. I have a few songs written." Although he wasn't sure he liked them. "And I'll be able to work once I'm moved." Wilson shifted on the sofa. "Don't you understand? I'm feeling dry and wrung out. The only time I felt good was when I was in Wyoming. I can write there, and I can't here, not anymore." The truth was, he'd been faking it for so long he wasn't sure he could do anything else. But he had to try, because what he'd been doing was no longer working. "I know you want me to be seen, but I don't want that. I need quiet." Wilson got up without saying anything more, knowing that at any minute Howard would pull out his phone and begin yapping.

Wilson walked to the sliding doors, pulled them open, and stepped outside the high-ceilinged white room and onto a balcony that overlooked the entire Los Angeles valley, with its long streets and buildings enshrouded in smog. After closing the door, he wandered around to the side of the house. He slipped off his shoes, sat at the edge of the pool, and dipped his feet into the warm water. This was probably the one thing he would miss—a swimming pool he could use year-round.

Closing his eyes and letting his mind wander, the sounds of the city faded until all he heard was the wind blowing past him. He was back in Wyoming, on his land, walking into his house, with Steve sitting in a chair on the porch. Steve stood up, lanky frame sidling up to him, those small hips swinging seductively. When he reached him, Steve placed his hands on Wilson's cheeks before kissing him hard and strong.

Wilson jerked himself out of his daydream and nearly fell into the pool. He shouldn't be thinking about Steve that way, even in his daydreams. Steve was an employee, and Willie Meadows could not have a relationship with another man. That would be the end of his career, and Wilson knew it. Yes, he was gay, he'd known that for years, but he couldn't act on it. Not after what had happened before.

"Willie, you okay?" Howard asked from behind him, and Wilson nodded before standing up, the water running down his legs and feet to pool on the hot concrete.

"I'm fine."

"The Realtor needs to speak to you. She says she has an offer on the house, and she sounded squealingly excited. Personally, I think she keeps calling just to get the chance to talk to you." After handing Wilson the phone, Howard walked away and picked up his own cell, and by the time Howard reached the door, he was already talking to someone.

"Hello, Helen," Wilson said.

"Morning," Helen said breathily, and Wilson rolled his eyes. He got that sometimes from women.

"I understand you have some news for me."

"Yes, I have an offer on your house, and they've agreed to the full asking price. They want it to be available in two weeks, however. Is that possible? That was their only stipulation. It seems one of the studios is setting up their latest star, and they need a suitable place."

"That's fine, Helen." He already had the movers on the way, and that would give him an excuse to get out of town even more quickly. "The sooner the better. Bring the papers by the house this afternoon, and I'll sign what you need, and we can get this done."

"Would you be willing to autograph something for me when I'm there? My niece is a huge fan."

"Of course, Helen. I'll be happy to." Wilson disconnected the line and set the phone on the table. Everyone wanted something here—even the people you paid to do things for you wanted a piece of you. At times, Wilson felt like they were taking tiny bites out of his soul each and every day. He picked up his shoes before walking into the house and up to his bedroom. On his way, he passed Maria, the woman who had been keeping house for him for the last eight years. "Maria, can I speak with you?" He walked into his office, and she followed, closing the door.

"Yes, Mr. Meadows."

"It's Wilson, and I have something I'd like to ask you. I'm sure you're aware that I'm selling the house. I'm planning to move to a ranch in Wyoming. I'll write you a sterling reference and provide you with a severance package, if that's what you'd like." He saw Maria go pale under her tanned skin. "But I'd like to ask if you'd consider moving with me to Wyoming. You'd keep house like you do here, but it's much smaller."

"You want me to cook for you too? I'm an excellent cook." The energy behind her question took Wilson by surprise. He really hadn't expected Maria to want to move with him. Then her face clouded. "You know I have a daughter, and I cannot leave her."

"Of course you can't. On the property, there's a small house that the manager stays in. You and your daughter would be welcome to use it, if you like. You'd have a place of your own, and you could be close to the main house. Think about it and let me know soon, okay?" Wilson smiled because he could see the excitement behind Maria's eyes.

Maria smiled and said in her Latina accent, "Thank you, Señor Wilson. I will let you know tomorrow." Wilson knew that Maria's daughter Alicia was five years old, and Maria had been trying to find a way for her daughter to go to a better school than the one she would have to attend if she stayed in her current neighborhood. Before deciding to move, Wilson had already been contemplating asking her to move into a section of the house with Alicia, but maybe this would work out better.

"Good. If you decide to come with me, I'll arrange to have your things packed and moved for you." Wilson figured it was the least he could do.

"Will Señor Howard be coming too?" She looked toward the door and bit her lip. Maria and Howard had never gotten along, probably because Howard was a slob and figured it was his right to have her clean up after him.

"No. Howard is staying here." Just saying that brought a certain amount of peace to his soul. He was coming to realize that he'd spent too much time with Howard over the years, and it was time for some distance. It seemed the rest of his household agreed with him, because Maria smiled a huge grin. "Let me know tomorrow, then."

Maria left his office without saying anything more, but Wilson was fairly sure she was going to come along. That was the last bit of business he'd needed to attend to here. There was finality in that thought, and it settled some of the nerves that had been fluttering inside him since his return. Wilson figured he would need to come back to LA on occasion, but he could stay in a hotel for those visits, especially since they would be working sessions.

A soft knock sounded on the door, and then Howard walked in. "I think we have an album deal." Howard settled into one of the chairs. "They're willing to pay even more than last time, but they want a lot of new material, as well as a few Western standards thrown in for continuity."

"Okay," Wilson agreed. "What's the catch?" There was always a catch. When the record company paid millions in advance in a deal, they always wanted something.

"In the studio, recording in three months," Howard said.

"Nine," Wilson told Howard, and he expected him to make a call, but Howard didn't move.

"I countered with a year, and they agreed to six months," Howard said with a self-satisfied smile, and Wilson let him have his moment. Howard was a good manager, and he knew what he was doing. "Can you do that?"

Wilson shrugged. "I have very little right now, so I don't know. What I need is inspiration, and I'm not going to find it here."

"I think I'm starting to understand that," Howard said.

"It's too easy to get caught up in the lifestyle here and forget what you're doing," Wilson said. "Think about it: I'm a Western singer who can't ride a horse and who's never actually seen the real West. I've been singing about wide-open spaces, crystal-clear water, rodeo, and cowgirls for almost a decade, and I've never really seen any of them. I'm a huge fraud and I'm starting to feel like one on the inside. That's why I bought the ranch, because I need to feel real. God knows I may hate it in the long run, but even the few days I was there were soothing for me."

"I worry about you being there alone," Howard said, and Wilson knew from his expression he was being sincere.

"I won't be alone. I'll make friends, and I think Maria is going to go with me. I know this is hard for you, too, but I need to do this."

"That's part of what concerns me. I don't want you being taken advantage of. Like it or not, I've been looking out for you for a long time, and I won't be there to watch over things. Like that kid at the ranch. It's not that I don't like him, I'm just wondering what he wants."

"Howard,"—Wilson's exasperation colored his voice—"I found him sleeping in one of the barn stalls because he had no other place to go, remember? He didn't even know who I was until I accidentally gave him one of the cards you had made up for me. I think Steve is going to be just fine." Truth be told, Howard's fears did have him wondering just a little what he would find when he got back. He wanted to believe the best in people, but his experiences had told him that wasn't always the wisest course.

"Don't worry about things here. I'll take care of everything," Howard reassured him, and Wilson was sure he would. They talked about business for a while, and then Howard left him alone. Wilson enjoyed the peace until it was time for lunch. After eating, the rest of his afternoon was busy with signing the deal to sell the house and making final arrangements to move. By the time he was ready for bed, Wilson was exhausted. He'd hoped he wouldn't spend his nights thinking of a certain cowboy sleeping in one of the rooms in his ranch, but he was finding that while he might be able to mostly repress his interest during the day, at night his mind ran free, and it seemed to keep running back to Steve in ways that left him sticky and wanting so much more than just dreams.

THE HOUSE was sold, and the movers had packed everything he wanted to take. Howard had found a place to live, but he was staying at the house to make sure everything was packed up and carted off to the auction house. In ten days, Wilson would sign the final papers, and then that portion of his life would be over. Now all that had to happen was the small plane he was riding in needed to get the hell on the ground so he could make the drive to the ranch. The ride had been bumpy for the past hour, and he was so ready for it to land. Maria and Alicia were in the row right behind him, and he could hear Maria talking softly in Spanish, trying to keep Alicia settled. Ten minutes later, they bumped down the runway and pulled up to the terminal. After getting their luggage, Wilson led them to his truck and soon they were on their way, with Alicia riding in the back of the supercab in her car seat.

"Everything is very different," Maria said as they rode. She spent the entire ride either looking out the windows or peering back at Alicia, who seemed full of questions.

"Will there be horses? Can I ride them? Will there be other kids to play with? What were the big animals by the side of the road?" Question after question poured out of the excited little girl, and Wilson answered the ones he could.

"Yes, we'll have horses, and probably a pony that you can ride. I'm not sure about kids, but we can ask the neighbors, although you'll probably meet some when you start school. And those were beef cows." Wilson answered the questions for round one, knowing that was just the beginning.

"Alicia, let Señor Wilson drive."

"It's okay," Wilson said with a smile and a wink at Alicia. "I'm glad she's excited. Just wait until you see snow," Wilson told Alicia, and he heard hands clapping and a squeal of girlish delight. Eventually the ride turned to questions of "are we there yet," and even those faded after a while until they passed through town. Both Alicia and Maria perked up as they continued to ride.

"There's so much space," Alicia said as they continued driving past fields dotted with cattle, the occasional house or barn rising in the distance and approaching slowly. As they got closer, Wilson felt himself getting nervously excited. After listening to

Howard for almost a week, he was beginning to wonder what he was going to find.

"This is it," he said as he slowed and made the turn into the drive. He jammed on the brakes, looking around to make sure he was in the right place.

"*Horsies!*" Alicia squealed from the backseat, and Wilson stared. There were indeed horses in the paddock, two of them, as a matter of fact. The house looked the same, and it was indeed his, but what the hell was going on, and where had those horses come from? Taking his foot off the brake, Wilson let the truck move forward. As he pulled into the parking space, he expected to see Steve around, but other than the horses, there was no movement in the yard. Looking around, Wilson saw a head peer around the barn door, and then Steve walked out, looking a bit pale.

Wilson opened his door and got out, staring quizzically at Steve, who slowly approached the truck.

"Did horses suddenly materialize out of nowhere?" Wilson tried to keep his voice light, but he was genuinely confused and worried about where these horses had come from.

"Wally and Dakota needed these horses trained, so they brought them over," Steve said, refusing to meet Wilson's eyes. "They're paying for me to train them, so I thought it would be okay. They also brought hay and straw for them, so the barn is all set up. So far they've been happy, and they said they'd tell other people about my training, so there may be more horses coming. I can tell them not to if that's what you want." Steve chewed his lower lip nervously, but his eyes, when he finally looked at Wilson, held such excitement there was no way Wilson could say no.

Wilson smiled, and Steve seemed to relax. "That's perfect, but don't take on more than you can handle, because we need to get a pony and some good riding horses in the next few weeks." Wilson was determined to learn to ride, and maybe once he got to know them better, he could ask Wally and Dakota to show him some of the ins and outs of working with cattle.

"I won't," Steve promised, and Wilson saw Alicia run around the front of the truck toward the paddock fence, with her mother right behind her. Steve followed them, looking at Wilson warily.

"That's Maria and her daughter, Alicia."

"Oh," Steve said softly looking at the house and then at the foreman's cottage. "I'll get my things moved out of the house, then." Steve walked toward the house. Wilson wondered for a few seconds what was going on, and then he realized what Steve must have thought he was seeing.

"Wait," Wilson said, and Steve stopped. When Steve turned around, Wilson saw the hurt in the young man's eyes. "You misunderstand, I think. Maria is here to keep house. She and Alicia will be staying in the foreman's cottage. Your room in the house is yours for as long as you want it. Hopefully in the next day or so, the truck will arrive with some furniture, including a bed you can use, if you like. I wish it were sooner, but I couldn't make them rush any faster."

"That's okay," Steve told him with what looked like a relieved smile on his face. "Do you want to see the other things I've done?" Steve looked as excited as a kid as he led Wilson around the ranch. "I cleaned up the ring. It was pretty good, but some weeds had started to grow, so I got them out of there. I also walked the paddocks and removed any weeds that might be harmful. Up near the house, there were some flower beds that haven't been used in a while. I cleaned those out, too, in case you wanted to have something planted, and out back there's a spot for what looks like a kitchen garden. It's too late to plant this year, but next year it could be used, if you want. Next, when I get time, I want to edge the drive and get the gravel out of the yard."

"You have been busy," Wilson said, impressed by Steve's initiative. "Were there any problems? You were alone quite a bit."

"No problems," Steve answered quickly, and Wilson saw that he wouldn't meet his eyes again. He knew something was going on, but Steve's expression hardened just before he turned away, and Wilson knew he wasn't going to get much out of him unless he pressed. He wasn't sure it was worth it right now.

"What's under the tarp?" Wilson asked as they walked around the back of the barn.

"My truck," Steve said. "I wanted to keep water out of the bed." Steve continued walking. "Oh, I found some old chairs in the basement, and I got them cleaned up. We can paint them, and they'll be really nice on the porch." Wilson knew he was being distracted, though he decided that for now, he'd give Steve his privacy while keeping his eyes open. Something wasn't quite right. Wilson got the idea that Steve was afraid of something.

Wilson's phone rang as he approached the house, and he tugged it out of his pocket, expecting to see Howard's number. "Hello," Wilson answered, seeing the strange number.

"Is this Mr. Edwards? We're about half an hour from your place, and we were wondering if we could deliver your things."

"Of course, bring them on by. We'll be on the lookout for you." Wilson hung up, thinking, *that was fast*. "The truck is on its way, so we need to be ready to help get it unloaded." Knowing that she was going to be cooking, Maria had directed the movers to pack up most of Wilson's LA kitchen. Wilson hadn't been expecting to have that much moved, but by the time Maria was done, the movers took a steady stream of boxes from the house.

"Your things won't be here until next week, so you and Alicia will be staying in the main house, if that's okay. If you'd be more comfortable, you're welcome to stay in a hotel in town." Wilson didn't want to push her.

"I wanna be near the horsies," Alicia pronounced, and that seemed to settle it for Maria. Everyone helped unload Wilson's pickup, getting their things placed in the various bedrooms before the moving van appeared. Wilson moved his truck out of the way, and the drivers maneuvered the van so the back nearly touched the front porch. The men got out and began unloading. At first they carried in boxes, with the kitchen filling up, and Maria got to work putting things away, with Alicia helping her.

Then they started bringing in the furniture. The bedroom sets came off first, and Wilson directed them to the proper rooms. He watched Steve's jaw drop open as a queen-size sleigh bed was set up in his room, with a matching dresser. "I never had anything this nice in my whole life," Steve said, and he got to work getting the furniture in place and the bed made up. Wilson's king-size bed came next, followed by another for what he figured would be an extra bedroom, but where Maria and Alicia would sleep until their things arrived. He was glad Howard had convinced him to take them all.

The pieces of living room furniture came next. There were just the saddle-leather sofas along with a few lamps, but the movers placed them before bringing in the rest of the things. The last thing they brought in was Wilson's humongous television. Once they were done, Wilson signed their paperwork, thanking them for their help, tipping both men before sending them on their way.

"Señor Wilson, you will need to get proper things," Maria said as she surveyed the room with what he knew was a critical eye. "But I am glad all the dead things did not come."

"So am I," Wilson agreed, sitting on one of the sofas. Maria hurried off, and Wilson heard her in the kitchen. Alicia raced down the hall, returning with a book. She looked around and approached Steve, reaching up to hand him the book. Wilson smiled when Steve sat on the other sofa, lifting Alicia next to him. When he opened the book, his eyes widened.

"I'm sorry, I don't read Spanish," Steve said, and Alicia looked at him with a pitying look. Steve opened the book and began to read as best he could, with Alicia correcting him. Wilson didn't think he'd ever seen anything more adorable in his life, especially when Steve would mess up one of the words really badly and Alicia would fill the room with giggles. Wilson couldn't keep his eyes off Steve, even though he knew he should, but that

ANDREW GREY

smile and the delight in his eyes when he read to Alicia was too wonderful not to watch. When he was done, Alicia climbed down off the sofa, and Wilson heard her run through the house again, before returning with a stuffed hippo. This time she curled next to Wilson, holding the hippo, and promptly fell asleep.

"Señor Wilson," Maria began as she walked into the room, and Wilson raised his finger to his lips. Maria took one look and rolled her eyes. "You two are going to spoil her, aren't you?" Maria questioned, looking alternately at Wilson and then Steve.

Wilson looked back at Maria, meeting her eyes. "Every chance I get."

Steve got up and followed Maria into the kitchen to remove the empty boxes and carry them outside. For the next few hours, Wilson sat with Alicia while the others worked. Eventually she shifted, and Wilson found a blanket and covered her, and then he too went to work.

Maria was a model of efficiency—she always had been—but Wilson saw it now in her unpacking. She had her kitchen whipped together in no time, and then she started in on his bedroom, making the beds. When he came in to unpack his clothes, she shooed him out of the room. Alicia woke up as he came through the living room, so he picked her up on his way and carried her outside to the ring, where Steve was working with one of the horses.

"Did Maria kick you out too?" Wilson asked as he stood at the fence, holding Alicia so she could watch. The light was beginning to fade, but Wilson could see that Steve had a lead on the horse.

"Can I ride him?" Alicia asked Wilson softly.

"Not yet," Wilson told her as they watched Steve work with the horse. "He still seems pretty wild." Steve called the horse to a halt and gave him something from his pocket before walking him out of the ring and letting the horse loose in the paddock. He then closed the gate, and Wilson wandered over with Alicia. "Why did Dakota bring these two over?"

Steve stood beside them, and they all watched as the horse bounded around his enclosure, looking for a way out. "He's pretty wild, and Dakota hasn't had any luck calming him down," Steve explained. "At first, he kept trying to bite me, but I stopped that pretty fast. Now he seems to test whatever enclosure he's in, looking for a way out."

"Why don't you bust him like they do in the movies? You know, ride him until he gives in?" Wilson asked, watching as the horse calmed down and began to eat.

"That's in the movies. I prefer to gentle them into the saddle." Steve raised his eyes to Wilson's and his hair caught the setting sun, glowing nearly red. "I would rather the horse learn to trust me than fear me. I want them to keep their spirit; that's part of what makes them unique and special. When you break them, you run the risk that they'll lose some of that spirit."

They watched the horses, and every time he inhaled, Wilson smelled horse and the land. He also got the occasional scent that drove his mind crazy, deep and earthy on top of rich, masculine musk that had Wilson inhaling deeply just for the slightest hint of it. And every time the scent was there, it sent a tingle through his entire body.

"Dinner is ready," Maria said from behind them, and Wilson turned as she took Alicia from his arms. "Go on in and eat," she told them both.

"Thank you," Wilson said, but he was reluctant to move. Wilson knew all he needed to do was move his hand a few inches and he could touch Steve's fingers. Part of Wilson urged him to do it, but he knew he shouldn't, for so many reasons. He knew it was going to be harder than he thought keeping himself from acting on what he wanted, but he had to. Steve worked for him, Willie Meadows couldn't be gay, and being with Steve could end his career. All those reasons played through his head, though they didn't mean a hill of beans when measured against the man standing next to him. Wilson turned and Steve did the same. They faced each other, eyes locking for a split second. Steve's pink tongue moved along his full lips, and Wilson's mouth relaxed, lips parting on their own.

"Dinner is getting cold," Maria said from the porch, and Wilson backed away, blinking to clear his head as he silently chastised himself for what he'd been about to do. Steve turned toward the house, and Wilson hung back for just a minute, turning away so he could adjust things in his pants and calm himself down. Looking out across the rangeland, he saw a truck coming down the road and noticed that it slowed as it approached the ranch. He watched as it continued coming closer, driving by relatively slowly but not pulling into the drive. Wilson thought he saw the driver watching the ranch, and he made sure they saw him watching them. He knew he was far enough away that they most likely wouldn't recognize him, so he stared back at the truck. Once it passed the drive, the truck sped away and eventually disappeared down the road.

Wilson waited until they were out of sight before turning and walking into the house. Maria had set up a makeshift table in the dining area, and Steve sat with a plate in front of him. Wilson went into the bathroom to wash up, still puzzling over the truck driver's behavior. He was probably imagining things, and they could have just been looking for someplace in particular. Wilson decided to file the incident away and, as he'd told himself before, to keep his eyes open.

As he joined Steve at the table, Maria placed a plate at Wilson's place, and he took a seat in what was probably one of the old porch chairs. Maria's enchiladas smelled inviting. "These are heavenly," he told Maria after taking his first bite. She continued fussing in the kitchen. "Maria, sit down and eat." She shook her head. "You and Alicia are part of the family here. Please come eat." She looked at him warily, but fixed a plate for herself and a small plate for Alicia. Steve must have scared up a bench from somewhere, because he slid over, and Maria sat down with Alicia next to her. "Let's get something straight. You all know who I am, and if you treat me like Willie Meadows, I'll fire you both." Wilson winked and smiled at both of them. "Here I'm just Wilson, and none of you are here to wait on me hand and foot. Maria, you'll take care of the house. This is your domain. If you want something, just ask, and I'll try to get it for you. The same goes for you," Wilson added, turning to Steve. "Now, there are some plans we need to make." He looked at Maria. "Tomorrow we're going into town to see about some furniture for this place, and we can get anything you think you need for the house."

"Thank you, Señor Wilson, I make a list," Maria said as she began eating.

"Steve, I need you to make a list of the gear and supplies we need for the barn and horses. We can get those in the next few days. I'm also thinking we need to find out when the next horse sale is being held because we should get a horse for you to ride and a pony." At the word pony, Alicia gasped and clapped her hands, forgetting about the fork in her hand.

"Eat, don't play at the table," Maria scolded lightly, and Wilson winked at Alicia.

"I'm not necessarily interested in making this a fully self-supporting ranch, but we should figure out what we're going to do with the land, and that I'm going to leave up to you," Wilson told Steve. "Come up with a plan, and we'll go over it." Wilson saw excitement in Steve's eyes. "Mainly, I want this to be our home." Wilson looked at each of them to make sure they understood he hadn't meant *his* home. He'd been surrounded by people all his life, but no place felt like home until he'd bought this piece of land. The others smiled and seemed to understand.

Wilson continued eating, and once he was done, thanked Maria for a wonderful dinner. He carried his dishes to the sink and rinsed them before placing them in the dishwasher. Then he walked through the house to his room, picking up his guitar. He carried it outside onto the porch, but there was nothing to sit on. He thought about going inside to get one of the old chairs, but just then the door opened and Steve carried one out, setting it down before returning with the other one a few moments later. Steve set down the chair, and then wandered over to the barn, leaving him alone. Wilson sat down and placed the guitar on his lap. He strummed the instrument, letting the sound enter his soul. That was how he'd always been able to write before. He kept strumming, letting his hands do what they wanted. Chord after chord flowed from the instrument, but nothing spoke to him. Instead, he settled into one of the songs from his last album. He closed his eyes and began to sing.

He got halfway through the song and stopped. It was one of his "country boy in the city" songs, and when he'd been in LA, that was how he'd felt, and that music had touched a lot of people. But right now, sitting on his porch with night descending around him, the sky filled with millions of points of light, the song felt hollow and as false as he'd felt the past few months. Wilson tried starting from the beginning again, but there was nothing there, no inspiration at all.

"Do you know where the Western songs came from?" Steve asked softly as Wilson set his guitar aside. Wilson could see him cutting the square of light that fell through the window. "They were sung around the campfire. One of the men would play the harmonica, or if the camp was lucky, a fiddle, and they'd all sing the songs everyone knew because they'd been passed from man to man and camp to camp."

"Are you saying I need a campfire?" Wilson asked as he looked into Steve's shining eyes.

"I'm not saying you need anything," Steve said, stammering slightly.

"It's okay. I haven't been able to write much in three months, and that's part of why I thought I needed a change of scenery." Wilson tried to keep the frustration that had been building that entire time out of his voice.

"So that's why you bought the ranch?" Steve asked, settling quietly into the other chair. "For inspiration?"

"Part of it, maybe." Wilson eased back into the chair, the old wood cradling him. "For a decade I've made my living singing Western music. Some of the songs I've written myself, and others are standards that I reworked and updated for a newer audience, and it's really worked. But I'm a fraud." Wilson closed his eyes so he wouldn't see the disappointed look on Steve's face. "I'm just some kid from Oshkosh who happened to be in the right place at the right time, with a voice that someone heard and thought would be perfect for Western ballads." Wilson opened his eyes, staring out into the darkness as bugs buzzed around the window, attracted by the light. "Now I'm supposed to write a dozen songs in a little less than six months and have them ready to go into the studio, but there's nothing inside." Wilson didn't move as he listened to the insects making their nightly calls. He could hear the horses walking and occasionally snorting in their paddocks. He was a fraud, and fear gripped him that the entire world was going to know it.

"I don't know how I can help, but I'll try," Steve said from next to him, and Wilson felt him touch his arm. He knew he should pull away, but that simple, concerned touch felt good.

"I appreciate that," Wilson said to the night, trying to keep himself and his feelings hidden despite the hand that almost felt like it was scorching his arm. He knew what Howard would do in this situation. He'd simply lock him up someplace until he produced the songs. That's what he'd done before, and it had worked, because without distractions, Wilson had been able to produce. But that wasn't going to work this time, and Wilson knew it. Thinking about that last time, Wilson began to chuckle.

"What's so funny?" Steve whispered, and Wilson turned to see Steve looking at him, his head cocked slightly in what Wilson interpreted as curiosity.

"Two years ago, I couldn't come up with any ideas either," Wilson explained. "Howard locked me in my office with a jug of water and bag of sandwiches. He said I could come out when I'd finished a song. Bastard kept me in there for six hours, but I walked out with the words and tune for 'LA Range'."

"What did you do after that?" Steve asked, and Wilson wished he could see his expression clearly.

"Raced to the bathroom," Wilson answered, and he heard Steve's laughter joining his. "But it broke the block, and more songs followed," Wilson added once their laughter died away. "I didn't feel as dry inside as I do now." Steve's hand had slipped away while they were laughing, and Wilson missed the touch. They sat quietly for a long while, companions, both seeming lost in their own thoughts. As time passed, Wilson became hyperaware of each movement Steve made. His scent seemed to settle around in the warm, still night air, and Wilson was very glad for the darkness, because the dick throbbing in his pants was at least hidden from view. Wilson kept repeating to himself the reasons why acting on this attraction he was feeling was a bad idea, but those arguments were beginning to sound as empty as he felt.

Standing up, Wilson said good night and went inside, walking toward his bedroom. The house was largely dark, and Maria's soft voice drifted down the hallway as she read to Alicia. Wilson went to his room and closed the door, getting ready for bed and wondering just how he was going to sleep knowing Steve was in the next room.

Chapter Four

STEVE SAT outside for a while thinking about things... well, mostly thinking about Wilson. When he'd touched Wilson's arm, Steve had felt a tingle go up his hand. He knew it was probably from simple excitement, but Wilson hadn't pulled away and Steve hadn't wanted to. Wilson had been very good to him, and Steve was beginning to suspect that Wilson was gay or at least curious. The way they'd almost kissed earlier had been a big giveaway. Granted, it could simply be his imagination, and Steve had to accept that. Wilson had turned him down twice. Even though Steve had thought he owed him, Wilson had still turned him down. Getting up from the chair, Steve walked through the now quiet house, turning off the lights as he went.

At Wilson's bedroom door, Steve stood still and listened, hoping to hear something from inside the room. He thought he might have heard Wilson moving around, but he couldn't be sure. He wasn't about to make another offer and get turned down a third time, so he quietly opened his bedroom door, walked inside, and closed it silently behind him. After undressing, Steve climbed into the bed Wilson had brought for him. The sheets were soft and the mattress perfect. He could hardly believe this was for him, and yet his mind wasn't really on the bed or the furniture, but on the man in the next room. He wondered if Wilson was asleep or if he, too, was lying in bed staring at the ceiling.

Steve shifted on the bed, rolling onto his stomach and groaning slightly as his cock slid against the soft sheets, sending a thrill up his spine. He'd been hard the entire time he'd been sitting next to Wilson, and he throbbed now as his mind pictured the object of his fascination lying in his own bed naked. The thought made him ache all the more. Rolling onto his back, Steve slid his hands down his stomach before skimming one along his length. Closing his eyes, he imagined that it was Wilson's hand gripping him firmly, stroking just the way he liked. Steve could almost hear Wilson singing to him in his deep, resonant voice as he touched him, and he wanted Wilson to touch him so damned bad. Stroking harder, Steve sank deeper into his fantasy. He could hear Wilson's voice washing over him the way it had outdoors when he'd heard him singing on the porch. Steve knew it wasn't so, but at the time he could almost feel like he'd been singing to him. It was a foolish notion, but one his desire latched onto readily. Stroking harder, he wondered what Wilson would feel like pressed to him, how his skin would feel under Steve's hands, what he'd taste like when he kissed him or when Steve sucked on his perky nipples. He didn't know much about what was under Wilson's clothes, but his imagination was pretty good, and he filled in all the details, including what Wilson's thick cock would feel like when it slipped into his body. That notion sent him over the edge, and though Steve tried to keep quiet, he wasn't sure he had as he writhed on the bed in an ecstasy of his own making that he sincerely wished he'd been able to share.

He stilled and waited to see if anyone had heard him, but he couldn't hear anything out in the hall, and after he wiped down his chest and hand on his dirty shirt, Steve settled into the bed, pulling up the covers in the air-conditioned room. He liked sleeping where it was cool, so he burrowed in and let the night take him.

Steve expected to sleep soundly, but all night long, images of Wilson kept running through his head. Waking or sleeping, the man seemed to continuously occupy his thoughts. The last time he woke, Steve saw the faintest amount of light starting to color the sky. He gave up trying to sleep and got up, dressed, and quietly left the house, heading out to the barn. There were chores to do and horses to tend. And a man to try to get out of his mind, although how he was going to do that was beyond him.

As Steve walked toward the barn, he heard a truck coming down the road, and he hurried inside the barn without thinking about it. They were still looking for him, he knew that. He'd seen their truck a few times, but he'd always managed to stay out of sight. Steve figured that pretty soon they'd decide he wasn't here. But what if they knew he was? If they'd spoken to people in town and someone had recognized him, they would know he was in the area. And if someone put together that he was with Wilson—that would explain why they kept driving by the ranch. After all, Steve knew his father wouldn't hire idiots to try to find him. Why couldn't the man just let him go? Scratch that. Steve knew the answer to that: David Peterson never let anyone or anything out of his sphere of influence if he could help it, and he usually could. Steve heard the truck zoom on by, and he breathed a sigh of relief as the horses wandered in from their paddocks, snorting as they picked up on his distress.

"I know," Steve said to Chester, the sandy-colored stallion that he had been working with a lot. He seemed to be responding more than Dakota's dark-brown young mare, Lilly, who was being extremely stubborn. Both horses were coming around, though; it would just take time. Chester butted his chest looking for a treat, and Steve knew that was the way to his heart. "You think I should tell Wilson, don't you?" The horse shook his head up and down as though he were answering, and Steve located a carrot from the package he'd brought out from the house. Steve hated the things with a passion, so when Wilson had added a huge package to the grocery cart before he left, Steve had brought them out to the barn. Giving one to each horse, he stroked Chester for a while before cautiously walking to Lilly to see what her mood was. She approached and let him stroke her nose. "I know you think I should tell him too," Steve said. "Maybe you have more sense than I do, but what if he doesn't want me around?" Lilly head-butted him as if to say he was being an idiot.

Stepping away, Steve got her lead and fastened it to her halter before opening the stall door and leading her out through the barn and to the ring. He might as well get something accomplished, since he was up, and working with horses always helped him think better. Once in the ring, he gave Lilly some exercise before tying her lead to a sturdy fencepost. Going back into the barn, he got the blanket and saddle that Dakota and Wally had brought over for her. Not making any sudden moves, he settled them over the fence and placed the blanket on Lilly's back. She turned to try to see what was happening, but didn't balk at the blanket, so Steve decided to try the saddle. His plan was to get her used to being saddled before ever trying to ride her. "It's okay, girl," Steve said in his most soothing tone, just above a whisper. He wanted her to strain to hear him—that way he would have her full attention. Lifting the saddle, he carefully placed it on her back and stepped away.

Lilly stood there and looked at him. She turned to gaze at the saddle before looking back at him again. Steve smiled and carefully moved closer, watching her closely for any signs of agitation. She looked slightly tense, but her muscles weren't twitchy, and she wasn't stamping.

"That's a good girl," Steve crooned in his keep-the-horse-calm voice. "I'm just going to tighten the girth a little." Steve kept one eye on Lilly and the other on the girth as he reached under her to bring the two halves together.

A snap from across the yard made Lilly jump. Hooves stamped around him. Steve tried to get away but lost his balance and ended up in the dirt. Scrambling, he tried to make it to the fence as Lilly bucked. The saddle went flying, and a hoof landed right next to his head. He heard a thump as the saddle hit the ground, the blanket landing on his chest. A hoof scraped along the side of his leg. Steve continued scrambling as Lilly bucked once again. Something grabbed his arm and pulled. Steve slid along the ground and under the fence.

"Are you hurt?" Wilson's deep voice cut through Steve's single-minded need to get away.

"Yes," Steve answered before he could think as pain shot up his leg. Steve grabbed his calf, but Wilson pushed his hand away and gently slid his pants up his leg.

"You're going to have a huge bruise, but there's no blood," Wilson said. Not that Steve even noticed the pain anymore with Wilson touching his leg so gently. He felt Wilson's hand move slightly, and Steve stifled a groan before slowly shifting and getting up. His leg throbbed, but he could stand and move. Gingerly, he picked up the blanket and saddle. Lilly simply stared at him, blinking her big eyes. Not one to give up, Steve began again with his soothing voice.

"Please make sure no one comes outside," Steve said in his horse-calming voice, and Wilson slowly walked toward the house. Soothing her with his voice and hands, Steve placed the blanket and saddle on her back. This time, she let him tighten the girth, and he untied her lead and walked her around the ring. As he walked Lilly, Steve saw that Wilson had returned and was leaning against the fence, watching them. Steve had a difficult time keeping his eyes off the other man, and after a while, he didn't try to hide his interest. He was a man, after all, and if Wilson truly wasn't interested, he'd let him know. But Steve was getting a little tired of the furtive glances, and he knew the way he'd felt when Wilson touched him, and the way he'd held Wilson's arm the night before, and how he'd had to force himself not to reach out and take the other man's hand. So the next time he walked by, Steve flashed Wilson a huge smile, and as he walked away, he made sure to add a touch of swing to his butt.

It had taken him a little time, but Steve was starting to remember who he was. Sure, he knew his father's minions were probably still out there looking for him, but he'd gotten away. He began walking just a little taller as he remembered that. It might have taken time and a considerable amount of anguish and hurt, not to mention what he'd done to survive, but he'd done it. He'd gotten out from under his father's fanatical control and made his way here. He didn't have to be proud of what he'd done to get here, but he was here, and that had taken courage and determination. At least that was what he told himself. And if he could do that, then he could get Wilson Edwards to notice him.

Steve pulled Lilly to a halt, and she stood where Steve wanted her. Bending down, he pretended to look at something on the ground. Steve smiled to himself when he thought he heard a groan from behind him. He wanted to look and see if Wilson was reacting, but forced himself to keep his mind on the task at hand. Lilly seemed to be cooperating, but he knew that could change in an instant with a horse as stubborn as she seemed to be. He straightened up and continued around the ring, Lilly walking calmly with the saddle on her back.

"Now that's something I never thought I would see." Dakota was standing next to Wilson as Steve approached that area of the fence. "Do you think someone will be able to ride her? She's been a mean cuss for as long as we've had her. Even Wally is wary of her, and the man keeps lions and tigers." Steve noticed that Wilson seemed surprised by that. "He runs a big cat rescue," Dakota explained to Wilson. "Actually, he runs a rescue for almost any kind of animal no one wants, except reptiles. I had to draw the line at slimy." Wally had shown Steve the animals while Wilson was gone, and Steve had found it fascinating until Shahrazad, one of Wally's tigers, tried to take a swipe at him.

"Yes. You'll be able to ride her," Steve said in answer to Dakota's question. "Chester is coming along well too. They need some time to trust again. Where did you get them?"

"There's a monthly auction on the other side of town. Their previous owner had a reputation for being hard on his horses, and I got them pretty cheaply. But none of us seemed to be able to get through to them."

"It's taken a week for her to allow a saddle to be placed on her back, and it may take a month before she'll allow any of us to ride her. Chester is probably a little ahead, but not too much. Give them time and I think they'll be fine." Lilly was getting antsy, so Steve began walking again, and she settled into a pretty easy rhythm. When he turned, he saw Wilson and Dakota talking earnestly, with Wilson looking intently at him. He got the distinct feeling that they were talking about him, and he wondered what Dakota was explaining so earnestly, but as he approached again, Dakota's voice fell off, and Wilson looked sheepish and appeared to be blushing.

"Would you like me to see if she'll let me walk her?" Dakota offered.

"Sure," he said in his horse-soothing voice. Dakota approached slowly and took the lead, and Lilly let him. Steve stepped back slowly, and Dakota walked her around the ring. Steve moved out of the ring and stood near Wilson. He watched Dakota for a while, but then got the feeling that Wilson was watching him. "Is something wrong?"

"Not sure," Wilson answered. "Dakota was explaining some things to me, and I think he's imagining things." Steve couldn't help a small snort. In the little time he'd spent around Dakota, Steve got the impression the man didn't miss much and that Wally was even more perceptive.

"What's that for?" Wilson asked with a touch of annoyance in his voice.

"What is it that Dakota said?" Steve turned toward Wilson, letting their eyes meet. This time, though, he let no hesitation show, leaving his desires as naked as the day he was born. Steve figured he might only get this one chance to let Wilson know that he was truly interested.

"That I," Wilson began, and Steve saw his mouth fall open, knowing then that his message had most likely been received. "That you...." Steve continued watching Wilson as he moved closer. Steve refused to close his eyes. If Wilson actually kissed him, Steve wanted to see everything and not miss a second of it. "I can't," Wilson whispered, and he began to pull away.

"You can," Steve countered hoarsely. "You can do what you want to do without worrying about anyone else."

"You work for me. I shouldn't. I...," Wilson stammered.

"Those are excuses." Steve took a step forward, and he could feel the heat rolling off Wilson's body. Steve wanted to reach out to touch Wilson's chest. "What do you want?" Steve asked. "If you could really have what you want... what is it?"

The air crackled between them, and Steve had no idea what Wilson would decide. Doubt and worry shone in his eyes, and Steve began to think he'd pushed too far. But then Wilson moved closer. Steve tilted his head slightly, and their lips met. Steve hadn't known quite what to expect. Fireworks, bells and whistles, that didn't happen. What he got was the most tender kiss he could have possibly imagined, firm yet incredibly wonderful. The bells didn't start ringing in his ears until he felt Wilson's hand in his hair, holding his head, deepening the kiss.

"I spent the last week wondering what that would be like," Wilson whispered when he pulled his lips away. "I kept seeing you every time I closed my eyes."

"Me too," Steve mumbled before pulling Wilson back into a kiss.

"Ooooh, kissing." Steve heard from behind him, and he jumped back. Alicia looked up at him, giggling like crazy. "You were kissing. Boys aren't supposed to kiss." She continued giggling and chanting as though she'd caught them doing something naughty, and Steve could almost feel Wilson's walls go back up.

"Alicia," Steve heard Maria say as she hurried across the yard. "You behave."

"But they were kissing," Alicia said indignantly.

"Yes, they were, and that's what some boys do when they like another boy," Maria explained as she lifted Alicia off her feet. "There's nothing wrong at all, and you need to be nice. Remember what we talked about last night? If you want to ride a pony you need to behave and act like a good girl."

Steve smiled at Maria, and she smiled back and winked.

"Now you say you're sorry."

Alicia looked down at her mother's feet. "I'm sorry," she said adorably, and then she looked first at Wilson and then at Steve. "You were kissing," she said again, and once again she seemed overcome with a fit of the giggles. Maria looked exasperated and tried her best not to notice.

"Breakfast will be ready in half an hour. Is he staying?" Maria asked as Dakota approached.

"Maria, that's Dakota. He and his partner, Wally, have a ranch a few miles from here," Wilson said, and Steve watched to see Maria's reaction, but she seemed to take it in stride.

"Dakota, can you stay for breakfast?" Wilson asked, and Dakota walked Lilly out of the ring and toward the barn.

"No, thank you. Wally's expecting me home." Dakota paused with Lilly. "You're doing a great job, Steve."

"Thank you," Steve said with a smile. "Just put her in the first stall, and I'll unsaddle her later. I want her to get used to having it on her back." Dakota and Lilly disappeared into the barn, and Dakota came out a few minutes later. Saying goodbye and waving, he walked to his truck.

Maria carried Alicia into the house, the little girl still giggling, and Steve turned to Wilson and waited. He really wanted a repeat of that kiss but wasn't quite sure how to ask for it, or if Wilson was going to simply walk away and pretend it hadn't happened. Instead, he started when Wilson reached down and took his hand. "I think you and I need to talk."

Steve wasn't sure he liked the sound of that, but he supposed talking was better than watching and lusting silently after each other. Steve agreed, and they walked together toward the house. As they approached, Steve saw a small face plastered to the glass, and he could almost hear Alicia telling her mother that he and Wilson were holding hands. As they approached the door, Wilson let his hand slip away, and Steve released a silent sigh before heading into the house.

Maria had set up the temporary table with a huge breakfast, and once she'd called Alicia to eat, they all sat down. Not meaning any offense to Maria's cooking, Steve really didn't pay much attention to his breakfast. He kept looking at Wilson all during the meal, and Wilson kept looking back. The air seemed to crackle between the two of them, and once, when he looked at Maria, she rolled her eyes at them. When he was done, Wilson got up from the table and took care of his dishes, leaving the house without saying a word. Steve was about to get up, but Maria touched his arm lightly.

"Señor Wilson is a very private man. He performs on stage all the time, but they don't know him. He is also afraid that if they do, no one will like him anymore. I work for him for eight years, and I see that he is not very happy there. I hope he will be happier here. But he must let himself be happy, and for that he needs time to decide for himself." Maria seemed to have said her piece, because she returned her attention to Alicia. "Now you eat. You are way too skinny." She placed some additional pancakes on his plate, and Steve began to eat.

After breakfast was over, Wilson took Maria and Alicia with him into town, and Steve worked with Chester. He kept an eye on the road as he worked with the horse, wondering more than once if he was looking for Wilson or the minions. He didn't have time to think about it much before he heard a vehicle approach and slow down, pulling into the drive. He didn't recognize it, and he didn't have time to make himself scarce. If it was the men his father sent, he was so screwed right now.

"Haven," he said when he recognized the cowboy he'd met first at the restaurant and then at Dakota and Wally's. "How's it going?"

"Pretty good," Haven answered as he walked over to the fence. "Is that Chester? He's looking good. I always thought I had a touch with horses, but that one gave me fits." Haven reached out and patted Chester's neck. "Sometimes he'd be responsive and others as stubborn as a mule."

"What brings you by?" Steve asked as he led Chester back to the barn. Haven followed, but, Steve noticed, not too closely, which was probably a good idea.

"Dakota forgot to give you all the invitation to the cookout they're having on the ranch in a few weeks. It was one of the reasons he came over, but he got wound up in the horses and totally forgot." Steve got Chester in his stall, and Haven reached into his pocket and handed Steve a piece of computer paper once he'd closed the stall door.

"Can I ask you something?" Steve inquired, and Haven nodded.

"Sure."

"Is it safe around here? You know, to be gay?" It was hard to ask the question, because he wasn't used to talking about things like that.

Haven shrugged slightly. "I suppose no more or less than anyplace else. Generally people are pretty accepting, though I have been in a few fights to protect myself or Phillip." Haven grinned wickedly. "The one man you want on your side in any fight is Wally."

Steve crinkled his brow. "Don't you mean Dakota?" He could see the big man being a terror in a fight.

"No. Wally is some sort of self-defense master. I've seen him bring down men three times his size with very little effort." Haven's expression relaxed. "I don't want to give you the wrong impression. While we have had trouble a few times, most people are understanding and accepting. It's not as though you're alone. Most people in the area know Dakota and Wally, or me and Phillip, and they know we're together. David and Mario are well liked, and there are others too. We're good members of the community, and we make sure people know it. I know Wyoming's got a bit of a bad rep, but I don't think it's any worse here than anyplace else. If anything, it's better."

"It couldn't be worse than where I come from," Steve commented, and he wished he'd kept his mouth shut because he could see the curiosity in Haven's eyes.

"Some people will have their opinion about what being gay is, and they're going to think what they want. I never told my father, but the son of a bitch would have killed me if he'd known. But Dakota's dad has always been supportive of him."

"My dad will never be supportive, not of this," Steve said. "But it doesn't matter, I guess, because like you said, he's going to think whatever he wants." Steve felt himself sinking into his own thoughts for a few seconds. "Sorry."

"No problem," Haven said with a smile and began walking toward the door once again. "I'll see you at the cookout if not before." Haven waved before leaving, and Steve heard his truck tires crunch on the gravel as he drove away.

Steve felt very unsettled. He knew he needed to tell Wilson about what was going on. He liked it here—it felt like a home to him, and he didn't want to have to leave. Steve left the barn and then immediately backed inside once again when he heard a vehicle approaching. This was getting ridiculous. He was afraid of his own shadow, and he couldn't live the rest of his life like this. Maybe it was just too dangerous for him, and for Wilson, Maria, and Alicia, if he stayed here any longer. The thought of leaving tore at his heart. Walking away from Wilson was the last thing he wanted to do.

The vehicle approached, and Steve waited. He heard it slow and then turn into the drive. Wilson pulled past the door, and Steve released the breath he'd been holding. This truly was ridiculous, and it needed to stop. Steve heard a truck door slam hard. He got busy in the barn as he heard heavy footsteps coming closer.

"Steve," Wilson barked harshly from behind him. Steve hadn't heard that tone before, and it made his heart fall into his boots. "I think you owe me an explanation." Wilson's eyes blazed hot with a fire Steve would have loved to see if it hadn't been accompanied by a hard expression and a mouth set in anger and hurt. Steve wasn't sure what to say, so he remained quiet. "There were men in town looking for you. They were being discreet, and at first I thought they might be reporters looking for me, but when I approached one of them near the hardware store, they didn't look at me except to show me a picture of you."

Steve's mouth went dry. "What did you tell them?"

"I said I'd seen you a few days ago and I gave you a lift to the interstate south of town. I'm not sure if they bought it, but they sure seemed to." Wilson's words became icy. "Now that I've lied for you, I think I deserve an explanation as to why these men are looking for you." Wilson took a deep breath, and Steve wanted to sink through the floor. "You told me no one was after you, and now I find this out. A lot of things have become clear, the way you've been hiding your truck and the way you seem to skitter away whenever someone comes around. Have these men been here?"

Steve nodded, remembering cowering under the living room window to stay out of sight. Wilson stopped talking and stared at him. Steve's first reaction was to run, get in his truck—he had a full tank of gas now—and get as far away as he could. "I was afraid you'd send me away if you knew."

Wilson's eyes softened, and Steve saw the lines on Wilson's face become less sharp. "Why don't you tell me what's happening, and I'll decide what I want to do." Wilson walked out of the barn and turned toward the house. Steve knew this was the moment where he had to decide if he trusted Wilson. Sure, he'd lusted after him, and he thought he was hot and stuff, but... Wilson had been good to him when no one else seemed to give a damn, not even the people he thought loved him. Feeling low, he figured it was time to face the music, so Steve slowly followed Wilson into the house.

Maria was working in the kitchen getting lunch, and Alicia sat on the living room floor playing with her toys, so Steve followed Wilson and stopped at the door to his bedroom. Wilson sat in the chair and motioned Steve toward the edge of the bed. "I knew we needed to talk, but I didn't think it would be about something like this. Who is it that's after you? Do you owe money to someone?"

Steve shook his head. That would be so easy to take care of in relation to this. "Those men are followers of my father, and I think they're trying to find me and take me home." Steve took a deep breath. "Look, Wilson, I never lied to you, not once. I never did anything wrong except for maybe getting caught kissing Kyle and admitting to my dad I was gay."

"So you've been hiding from these men for how long?" Wilson asked, his voice coaxing but firm.

"I first saw them just after you left. I hid from them, and they didn't see me, so I hoped they would think I was someplace else. Someone must have told them they saw me around town, because I've seen them drive by a few times." Steve stared at the floor, unable to look at Wilson. He'd been so happy after Wilson had kissed him, and now that was gone and would probably never happen again.

"I think I have too," Wilson said. "Why would they keep looking for you?"

"Because my dad is afraid for my soul, or at least that's what he says," Steve tried to explain, but he knew he was making a mess of it.

"So your dad's a minister?" Wilson asked, and Steve shook his head.

"He's a cult leader. He likes to think he's a minister watching over his flock, but he controls the lives of everyone at the compound. I saw a report on the news about us once when I snuck off to watch television. At first I thought that the report was falsified by the government and the 'liberal media', as my dad says." Steve tried to keep his voice as level as he could. "About six months ago, my dad caught me with another boy. We'd only kissed, but he flew into a rage and locked me in a small room. I don't know how long I was in there, but I fell asleep on the floor, and I woke up in what they said was a hospital." Steve felt his throat begin to tighten. He remembered the fear of waking up tied to a bed and not knowing anyone or anything. "They must have drugged the little bit of food they gave me, but I don't remember anything between the dark room and the 'hospital.' After I woke fully, a huge man came into the room, and he untied me and helped me out of the bed and down the hall to what looked like a prayer meeting." Steve clamped his eyes closed and felt himself begin to shake. To his surprise, he felt the bed dip, and Wilson wrapped his arms around him.

"You don't have to go into anything about that if you aren't ready. Just tell me why your father has men looking for you," Wilson prompted, and Steve tried, but he continued shaking as fear engulfed him. He knew if his father got ahold of him, he'd end up someplace worse this time, and that "hospital" had been terrifyingly bad.

"He never lets any of his followers leave. He says it's for the benefit of their souls, but I know now that it's only because that gives him the power he craves. He completely controls the life of everyone at the compound, and his word is law as far as his followers are concerned." Steve stopped shaking, but Wilson didn't let go. "After about a week at the hospital... facility... whatever you want to call it, I decided to go along with them. So I answered their questions the way they wanted and played their little games. I didn't fight or anything, and when they allowed me more freedom, I took it. After another week, I made a run for it. I had a little money Dad didn't know about that I used to buy the truck, and I headed up here. I'd wanted to get away from Dad's minions for a while, so I'd written for a job, and Mrs. Henfield offered me one. They must have read my mail at the hospital. I know the men after me are some of Dad's followers, and they won't stop until they find me because they're just as fanatical as Dad."

"How did you meet Mrs. Henfield?" Wilson asked.

"I didn't really. I wanted to get away and that meant a job, so I snuck out a few times and went to the library where they had computers. I saw an ad on a horse training website and answered it. It took a while because I had to be careful."

Steve stood up, Wilson's arms slipping away. He couldn't look at Wilson as he thought about what he'd done to try to keep some food in his stomach and gas in the tank so he could get as far away from Texas and his father as he could. "Somehow I made it here on fumes without eating for almost two days, and that's when I met you." Steve walked toward the door, turning back and opening his mouth to say something, but it would have sounded dumb, so he pulled open the door and walked across the hall. Inside the room Wilson had given him to use, Steve opened the closet door and retrieved his old duffel.

Chapter Five

WILSON SAT on the edge of the bed, watching Steve leave the room. Shock over what Steve had told him had him shutting down. How could Steve's father, or anyone's for that matter, do that? He'd actually thrown Steve away because he wasn't good enough or didn't measure up to some standard, because he was gay. Wilson stared at his bedroom door. Steve was wonderful, and his father had dismissed him out of hand. Closing his eyes, Wilson tried to get Steve's hurt look out of his mind.

Wilson's eyes snapped open. That look, it wasn't for his father—it was for him. Steve was leaving, and the notion scared him and spurred him to action. Wilson jumped up and hurrying into the hallway, he saw that Steve's door was closed. He heard Steve moving inside, and relief flooded into Wilson's mind that he wasn't already gone. Wilson turned the knob and pushed the door open. Steve stood near the foot of the bed with his old canvas bag in his hand. When Steve looked at him, Wilson's heart ached. Steve looked lost, and he lifted the bag as though he needed to cover himself. "Steve, don't go," Wilson said plaintively.

"You'll be safer if I do," Steve said, but he didn't make a move to begin packing. "They aren't going to stop looking for me. Dad has gotten it into their heads that finding me is some sort of religious calling, and they'll look forever if they have to."

Wilson moved further into the room. "I don't want you to leave." The thought of Steve leaving made his heart pound and every particle of his being scream not to let him go. What it was about this man that got to Wilson, he wished he understood, but he definitely knew that if he let Steve go, he'd not only regret it, but he would be missing something vital in his life. Wilson still wasn't sure what that meant, or if he was really ready for a relationship with another man. Fuck, he didn't know shit, and he knew it. Wilson felt lost, and he grasped at the one person who helped make him feel less lost. His music, the one thing that had sustained him through his loneliness, seemed to be silent, and the desires he'd suppressed for years were coming to the surface, leaving Wilson a little puzzled by it all.

"I don't want to. But it would mean that everyone here would be safer." Steve lowered the duffel and finally let it drop to the floor. "You've been nice to me, and I don't want anything to happen to you because of that."

"Nothing will. But I think you need to stop hiding. If these men come around again, we'll deal with them. You can't live your life diving into the barn every time a vehicle comes down the road." Wilson saw Steve agree, and he moved closer. "As for the rest, I don't know what to do."

"The rest?" Steve asked, and his eyes widened and regained a bit of their sparkle as Wilson moved closer still. "Oh, that rest."

"Yes," Wilson agreed, stopping. "You know who I am and what it would cost me to let everyone know I'm gay. But it's also just a matter of time before people find out where I am. Then reporters will begin snooping around, and God knows what else, especially if what I'm feeling for a certain cowboy comes out in the open." Wilson was lonely, he knew that, but he thought that what he felt for Steve was more than that, a lot more, or at least it could be. "I'm afraid and I'm willing to admit it."

"I understand about fear. I lived with it for months. The entire time I was in that facility, my father visited me one time, and that was only to ask me if I was ready to be a human being and stop acting like an animal. I actually stood in front of him and told him that I was gay, not an animal. I thought he was going to hit me, but he turned away instead. He stayed for a total of fifteen minutes. So I understand fear, but before I ran, I had to decide if taking my chances with the unknown was better or worse than spending months in a facility where they tried to change me into something I could never be. And you know what I found out?" Wilson shook his head. "The fear is worse than the reality. I had no idea how I was going to survive away from the community, where I'd lived surrounded by people I'd known almost my whole life."

"Was your father always that controlling?" Wilson asked, reaching to take Steve's hand, rough and strong from work.

"He got worse once my mother died, or at least that's what some of the people in the community told me. They were beginning to worry themselves, but no one would stand up to my dad. As far as I know, I'm the first person to actually leave the community," Steve explained, and Wilson felt Steve squeeze his hand. "Well, other than Kyle. He's the boy I kissed, and I have no idea what happened to him. I never saw him again, not even in the facility." Definite sadness colored Steve's voice.

"Do you love him?" Wilson asked, surprised at the pang of jealousy that shot through him. It had never occurred to Wilson that Steve might love someone else, and the idea made his head throb. Without thinking, he tightened his grip on Steve's hand.

"I don't think so. I've known Kyle for a long time, and he was a friend. After a while, we both sort of figured out that we liked the same things... if you know what I mean. We did stuff together, but it was always hurried, the moments stolen. We were both so scared of being caught, but that's what happened anyway." Steve sighed loudly. Wilson knew Steve hadn't told him everything, but it was enough for now. Steve looked tired, and he was probably a bit drained.

A soft knock on the door pulled their attention away from Steve's story, which seemed to relieve the younger man. Wilson opened the door to find Maria standing in the doorway. "I know it's late, but I made some lunch."

"Thank you, we'll be right out," Wilson said, and he saw her look at Steve, still sitting on the edge of the bed. He knew she wanted to ask, but she simply nodded, and Wilson closed the door once again.

"Is there anything else you want to know?" Steve asked, and Wilson walked to where he sat, taking his hand.

"Only if there's something you want to tell me. I know there's more, I can see it in your face, but if you're not ready to tell me, that's okay." Wilson had gotten the information he needed from Steve to help protect him and the ranch, and that was all he needed. "You're allowed your secrets, if that's what you want."

Steve lifted his eyes from where they'd been studying his shoes. "It's just, the...." Wilson wasn't sure what he was seeing— pain, shame, maybe some mixture—in Steve's eyes, but it almost made him take a step back.

"It's okay. When you're ready you can tell me." Wilson sat on the bed. He'd asked Steve to tell him about his past, so Wilson figured he should come clean too. "I met someone a few years ago. His name was Clay, and I thought he cared for me. But he didn't. All he cared about was being with Willie Meadows and what he could get." Wilson felt Steve shift, and then he was being hugged, hard.

"The only person I care about is Wilson. Whatever he did to you, this Clay was a jerk if he couldn't see who you really are." Steve brought their lips together, and Wilson stopped thinking about anything else—he never wanted this to end. And to think less than half an hour earlier, he'd almost let Steve go. Steve slid his tongue along Wilson's lips as if asking for entrance, and they parted almost on their own. Wilson wanted Steve badly. His pants hurt, they were so tight, and he felt his cock throbbing in time with his racing heart. Steve slid his fingers around the back of his neck, deepening the kiss as Steve seemed to take what he wanted, and Wilson gave, because he wanted the same thing. All his worries and concerns momentarily slipped away as they feasted on each other's lips, each gasping when they came up for air, only to begin again.

"We should eat and get the truck unloaded," Wilson said during a break, breathing deeply and swallowing hard as Steve stared deeply into his eyes. Steve nodded, smiled, and then began kissing him again. Wilson went with it. Eventually they did make it to lunch, with Maria staring daggers at both of them even as Wilson could see her lips threatening to turn up into a smile.

FOR THE next week or so, the ranch was very quiet. Maria's things arrived, and they got her settled. The furniture that Wilson had bought was delivered, and the house seemed even more like a home. The hardest part for Wilson were the nights, when he'd lie awake listening to the house. So many times he wanted to knock on Steve's door, but something always held him back. They kissed and touched a lot, but they had never gone any further than that. There was visible evidence that Steve was more than ready to go further, and Wilson knew the reason they hadn't was because of him. Wilson knew he was afraid. Some people in town knew who he was, and though they largely left him alone and gave him his privacy every time he came to town, Wilson knew he was being watched. Innocently, but watched nonetheless. So he'd stayed in his room and kept his hands largely to himself, which was definitely beginning to get a little old.

"Today's the auction, right?" Steve asked him as he was walking Lilly from the ring to her paddock. She was completely taken with Steve, and had even taken to him inserting a bit without too much fuss and only one bite mark.

"Yes. We need to leave in the next half hour," Wilson said, and Steve finished up what he was doing. After making sure everything was set—Steve was becoming a mother hen to those two horses—he was waiting by the truck when Wilson walked down the porch steps.

The ride to the auction took about half an hour. Dakota and Haven had agreed to meet them there and had even offered the use of their trailer to bring home any of their purchases. Steve seemed "jump out of his skin" excited, and as soon as they arrived, he disappeared into the barns to look over the stock.

Wilson wandered through the barns, catching up with Steve as he was standing near one of the stalls that held a blond horse that was already nuzzling Steve's pocket, looking for treats. "This should be a great riding horse. He's friendly and seems to have a great nature."

"What about a pony for Alicia?" Wilson asked, and Steve led him to that section of the barns. Together they looked at the ponies, but Wilson had no idea what to look for, and he let Steve take the lead. Steve picked out two ponies that he thought would work.

The auction was starting, so they followed the auctioneer as he began at one end of the barn. He talked so fast Wilson could barely understand him as he pattered for bids. But Wilson got the hang of it before they reached the first of the ponies they were interested in. Wilson bought the pony, and he could almost hear Alicia's squeals and giggles when she saw her.

"Now, here we have a wonderful horse. He's older but perfect for someone learning to ride. Great disposition and just loves attention." The horse tried to nuzzle the auctioneer's hat, and he stroked his nose with a smile. As soon as the auctioneer began, Wilson raised his paddle to bid.

Steve nudged him. "What is this horse for?"

"We have someone who needs to learn to ride," Wilson said as he raised his paddle to place another bid, trying to divide his attention between the auctioneer and Steve.

Steve stopped and turned, looking at him strangely. "Who, Maria?"

Wilson leaned close to Steve. "Me," he whispered, and Steve's eyes widened.

"You don't know how to ride?" Steve asked quietly, and Wilson shook his head. "Then who is the other horse for?" Steve looked back to where the blond quarter horse had been housed.

"I figured you'd need a horse to ride," Wilson answered, and the smile he got in return was nearly blinding. He heard the auctioneer calling for another bid and he raised his number. The auctioneer took the bid, and there were no more after that. The hammer came down at a good price, and Wilson had just bought a horse that would be his very own. It took a while, but eventually they arrived at the final horse that Steve had chosen, and he seemed to be one of the stars of the day.

"A quarter horse stallion of impeccable breeding," the auctioneer began, "an asset to any stable." He went on and on, and Wilson was beginning to wonder what this horse was. The bidding began, and when the auctioneer mentioned the starting price, Wilson looked to Steve and he saw him swallow hard. Obviously he hadn't expected him to start at that high a price. Wilson raised his paddle and continued bidding. One by one, the other bidders backed away until it was only Wilson and another man, who looked equally determined.

The woman next to the other bidder nudged her husband. The room had gotten quiet as everyone wondered just how high the price would go. "Dear, you're bidding against Willie Meadows!" The woman's voice carried all through the sale, and the man's paddle didn't rise again after Wilson bid one last time, and then the horse was his. Wilson was shaking a little with excitement, and Steve looked up at him in complete astonished admiration.

"What are you going to do with him when you get home?" Dakota asked as he and Haven joined their circle. "You certainly made a splash in the horse scene here, buying the star of the day."

All three of them looked at him, and Wilson began to laugh. "I bought him so Steve would have something to ride. I didn't realize he was going to cost so much." That should teach him—next time he'd spend more time on the research. "I'll go pay the bill and complete any paperwork that's needed, and we can get the horses loaded." What he was going to do with a $30,000 horse was truly beyond him, but he'd just bought one.

Wilson threaded through the people and made his way to the auctioneer's office area. The sea of people seemed to part ahead of him, and he saw people whispering and mumbling to each other. He definitely should have thought this through before making an appearance like this. He'd kept a rather low profile, but now he was going to be on the lips of every person in town. Wilson knew that was going to happen sooner or later, but he'd hoped it would be later. Reaching the desk, he explained who he was, and the woman looked up from her paperwork and instantly blushed. "It's okay, darlin'," Wilson said in his best accented voice. "I'm just like anyone else." She made out the paperwork, and Wilson signed it before handing her his credit card. She looked at it a few times and then up at him.

"I don't know what this is," she said softly.

"Do you take American Express?" Wilson asked, and she nodded. "That's a black card. It'll go through." Hell, Wilson could charge a Gulf Stream on it and it would go through. She nodded and ran the card through, and a few seconds later, Wilson's phone rang. It was the credit card company. After asking a few questions, the charge was approved, and Wilson signed the slip. Just like that he owned three horses, and by the time he returned, Dakota, Steve, and Haven were in the process of loading the horses into the trailer, along with the one that Haven had purchased, and soon they were on their way.

"I can't believe I picked out the most expensive horse in the place," Steve said once they were on their way back. Wilson nodded and kept his eyes on the horse trailer ahead of them.

"You saw quality and went for it," Wilson said with a smile. "So where did you learn to work with horses?"

"The community started out as a back-to-nature commune, so a lot of the work was done with horses. There weren't a lot of cars and heavy equipment." Steve looked out the side window. "That was how it started out. It was always religious, but at some point my dad began to take over, and things got more and more fanatical. From what I can gather, the change was so gradual that most people didn't realize it was happening until it was too late." Steve turned to look at him again. "Sorry, I got off track. Everyone in the community had a job to do, and mine was working with the men who took care of the horses. I started when I was eight, and it lasted until my father threw me into that tiny, cold, concrete room."

Wilson stomped on the brakes, nearly throwing both of them through the windshield. "He what?" Wilson nearly shouted, and Steve flinched and moved away. "Your father did what to you?" he asked, once a bit of the shock wore off. "He threw you in a tiny room?" Steve nodded, and Wilson tried to get control of his breathing. His pulse raced, and Wilson gripped the steering wheel so tight his fingers hurt.

"After my dad found out I was gay, he locked me in an underground concrete room. I told you about that," Steve said in a small voice. "There was no light, and I was so cold even in the Texas spring."

"I thought he'd locked you in your room, not in some small hellhole." Wilson forced himself to breathe. "I'm mad at your father, not you. No parent should ever do to their child what he did to you." Wilson heard a horn from behind him, and he began to move once again, some of his anger dissipating, but not his determination to see that man punished somehow. "And that's what you think those men looking for you are trying to drag you back to?"

Steve nodded, his eyes filling with fear. "I think so. My dad's a fanatic, and so are they."

Wilson wasn't sure what to say, but he wasn't letting anyone take Steve where he didn't want to go. The men Wilson had seen hadn't been around again, and he was cautiously optimistic, but not fully ready to declare that they were gone for good.

THEY ARRIVED back at the ranch and unloaded the horses to squeals of delight as Alicia saw the pony.

"When can I ride her?" Alicia asked, excited.

"We have to get a saddle for her and make sure she's okay before you can ride her," Steve said, looking at Wilson.

"I'll have Wally come over to make sure there aren't any issues with any of the horses, but they all look healthy to me. You can head in to the Spring's Tack and Saddle—they should be able to fix you up with everything you need for all the horses," Dakota said as he and Haven carefully unloaded the last of Wilson's purchases, and Wilson watched as the horse he'd learn to ride on was led into the barn.

"Did you want me to teach you to ride?" Steve asked from behind him.

"I was hoping you would," Wilson answered with a smile as he saw Alicia jumping up and down near the pony. Haven lifted her onto the pony's back, and she instantly hugged the pony.

"Of course," Steve said. "We can start as soon as we get all the gear." Steve flashed him a smile and then walked into the barn to make sure his new charges were all settled.

Maria had lunch ready soon after. Dakota and Haven joined them for lunch, and everyone had a great time talking around his new table. It was the first time the table had been filled, and Wilson hoped it wasn't the last.

"I'm done, Mama," Alicia said after two bites, getting up from the table and hurrying to the window.

"You know she's going to want to sleep in the stall with that pony," Dakota told Maria, "because I did with my first one, and I wasn't much older than her."

Maria scoffed and then looked at Alicia, who had her face plastered to the window. "Don't even think about sleeping with that pony," Maria scolded lightly but firmly, and Wilson could see Alicia's face fall. He chuckled, and the rest of the men did as well, because they all knew Dakota had been right.

After lunch, everyone helped clean up, with Dakota and Steve doing the dishes. Maria only reluctantly left her kitchen. Once everything was cleaned up, Dakota and Haven headed out, and Steve went to the barn. Wilson grabbed his guitar and sat on the porch, once again trying to feel inspired. A lot had happened over the past week, and every day he was feeling more and more content in his skin, but try as he might, the music wouldn't come, so instead he began to play some of the old standards. Pretty soon he was singing, low and soft, almost to himself.

He hadn't noticed that Steve had joined him until he heard a medium tenor voice join him in the song. "Sorry," Steve said when Wilson stopped.

"Don't be, you sound really nice," Wilson said before beginning to play again. Motioning toward the other chair, he saw Steve sit next to him, and they began to sing. Steve was tentative at first, but after a while, he got stronger and his voice blossomed, melding with Wilson's in beautiful harmony. When the song ended, Wilson began another, and Steve sang right along. This felt so right, so perfect. The door opened near them, and he saw Maria and Alicia sit together on the bench, with Maria holding her daughter on her lap as they listened.

He and Steve sang until Wilson heard Steve's voice get tired, and then he brought their sing-along to an end.

"That was fun," Steve said with a grin, and Wilson nodded his agreement, putting his guitar aside. "Did you get any ideas?" Wilson thought for a few seconds and then shrugged. "Then how about we measure the horses and go get some saddles? I'll even drive," Steve said with a grin.

THE SADDLE store was perplexing for Wilson, but Steve seemed to know exactly what they needed, and they arrived back at the ranch at dinnertime with the truck full and Wilson's wallet lighter. The man at the store had fallen all over Wilson to help him and had even called him Willie a few times. "I'm just another guy like you. Please call me Wilson," he'd said when he extended his hand after paying for their purchases. "Out here I just want to be me."

The man helping them, who'd introduced himself as Jake, nodded once. "That's cool. We've never had anyone famous out here before."

Wilson smiled his usual smile. "Just treat me like you would anyone else, no better and no worse. I want to be a part of the community," Wilson had said, and that seemed to sit well with Jake. He helped them load all their purchases into the truck.

"I suppose," Jake said once they were loaded, "that treating you like everyone else doesn't mean I can't ask for an autograph. My sister would just die."

"I'll be back, and if you want to bring in a CD, I'll sign it for her." Wilson shook Jake's hand while Steve fussed, making sure everything was secure in the truck. With a final wave, they pulled away, heading for the ranch.

Clouds had been rolling in, and by the time they pulled into the drive, thunder rolled across the range. Wilson parked near the barn, and Steve jumped out. "I need to get the horses inside," Steve said, grabbing a saddle from the back and carrying it into the barn. As Wilson followed with another saddle, he saw Steve leading the horses into their stalls. "It's going to be bad."

"How can you tell?" Wilson asked, setting the saddle next to the other before going back for the third.

"The horses are agitated and about two seconds from bolting," Steve said, closing the stall door and rushing back out. The wind was picking up as Wilson reached into the truck and lifted out the small pony saddle. Wilson heard Chester stomping and snorting in his paddock, and he looked toward the horizon where a line of black seemed to be getting closer and closer. Wilson hurried inside with the saddle before rushing back outside for the rest of the things. The wind continued building, and he had to pull off his hat so it wouldn't blow away. He got the last of the things inside as Steve brought in another horse. "There's still two to go."

Wilson followed Steve outside, opening the gate to the pony's paddock, and led her into the barn. He wasn't sure which stall was hers, so he waited for Steve, who pointed, and he guided her inside. They made sure all the horses had hay and water before hurrying back outside.

The sky was black as coal, and Steve kept looking to the west as he scampered for the house. Wilson got in the truck, pulling it to his spot before racing to the porch. The wind was whipping, and Steve stood just under the eaves, looking to the west. "Get inside!" Wilson yelled as he opened the door, a gust of wind threatening to take the storm door out of his hand.

The deafening sound lessened once they were inside. Maria was in the living room with Alicia, trying to keep her calm, but it didn't seem to be working.

"It's going to be fine. The rain will be here soon," Wilson soothed as he turned on the television. There were all kinds of warnings rolling across the bottom of the screen, but Wilson wasn't sure which ones affected them because he wasn't sure what county they were in.

"Hear that?" Steve said, and everyone got quiet.

"Sounds like a train," Maria commented, continuing to rock Alicia.

"That's no train! That's a twister! Get in the cellar now!" he cried, grabbing Alicia from Maria and heading toward the basement. Maria followed, and Wilson brought up the rear, closing the door behind them before descending the stairs. He made it to the bottom before the lights went out and the sound got louder. Alicia was crying, holding onto Steve, and Wilson wished he could do the same thing.

Wilson listened as the sound continued. He heard something bang upstairs and felt the entire house shake and quiver around him. Then the sound began to dissipate, and after that, all he heard was his own heart beating in his ears. Steve handed Alicia to Maria and carefully made his way up the stairs. There was almost no light, and mostly Wilson only heard Steve as a dark figure climbed the stairs. The light increased when Steve opened the door, but it dimmed again when he closed it.

Wilson heard Steve moving around above them, and then the door opened once again. "The house looks fine. The windows seem to be intact, and the barn and your truck are still there. I don't know what that thump was, but it's raining too hard to find out now, and there's no power or phone."

Wilson picked up his cell, and thankfully, he was able to get a signal. He looked through his numbers and placed a call to Dakota, who answered.

"Are you okay?" Wilson asked before saying hello.

"Yes, we seem to be. You?"

"Yeah," Wilson answered. "The house, barn, and other buildings seem to be standing." Something thudded lightly on the roof, and Wilson looked out the window. White stuff was raining down, and at first Wilson thought it was hail, but then it was joined by pink and brown bits. "I think someone wasn't so lucky. We've got what looks like pieces of building material coming down." Wilson continued watching, but the rain of debris seemed to have stopped.

"Let me call around and see what's going on. Twisters can lift stuff into the air and set it down miles away. We've got some stuff on the ground too." Dakota disconnected. Steve had already helped Maria and Alicia up the stairs. Wilson watched out the windows as the rain began to taper off. Walking to his room, Wilson rummaged in his closet and found a large umbrella.

He and Steve made their way under it to the barn. The yard was a muddy mess, strewn with bits of debris. They got to the barn, and it seemed dry. The wind had blown open one of the doors, and Steve began cleaning up the mess, but the horses were all fine, munching away in their stalls. The saddles and other purchases were where they'd left them in their hurry, and Wilson began putting them away, feeling extremely relieved. Once he was done, he stood in the doorway watching as Steve's hips swayed when he pushed the broom, and the way his hair caught the light as the sun's rays broke through the retreating clouds. Stepping closer, Wilson saw Steve smile at him as he worked. Wilson opened the door at the back of the barn and looked out. In the distance, he could see where the ground had been torn up, the worst of the storm passing to the north. "Are the horses okay?"

"They're fine," Steve said from behind him, and Wilson turned around to see the horse he'd purchased earlier nuzzling Steve's chest. "Is Maria's place okay?"

"It appears to be. Looks like we were lucky." Wilson saw bits of debris scattered in the fields for as far as he could see.

"We'll have to clear the paddocks tomorrow. The trash could be dangerous for the horses." Steve stood so close Wilson could almost feel the heat from his body. Steve's scent was nearly overpowering, and with every breath it got stronger. Steve had known exactly what to do and he'd taken charge. If the tornado had come any closer, he would have saved all their lives with his quick thinking. Moving closer, Wilson stroked Steve's cheek, and as Steve turned toward him, Wilson tasted the sweetest lips he could ever have imagined.

The broom handle hit the concrete with a snap, and then Steve wrapped his arms around him, holding tight as their kiss deepened. Wilson could feel Steve's desire rolling off him in waves as physical evidence pressed against Wilson's hip. "I've wanted you since that first night I saw you," Steve said softly, and Wilson stopped, pushing back slightly.

"You don't owe me anything, if that's what you're thinking." He didn't want this to be about Steve thinking he was paying some kind of debt.

"I know. You wouldn't let me do that, and I'm so grateful." Steve pulled him close once again. "I was wrong to make that offer before, but I thought...." Wilson pressed his finger to his lips.

"I know," Wilson said, and Steve's eyes widened. "Not the details, but I know you did things to survive that you aren't happy about. I just want to make sure this isn't one of them."

"It's not. It never was," Steve told him, and Wilson's throat began to close, and he blinked a few times because his eyes were getting watery. Then he hugged Steve tight, their lips meeting once again. Wilson felt Steve vibrating in his arms, and he ran his fingers through Steve's silky hair. When they took a break from kissing, Wilson buried his nose in Steve's beautiful curls, inhaling deeply the scent of hay and the wind, as well as Steve. Wilson never wanted to let him go, and when Steve tilted his head, Wilson looked into his deep eyes and then kissed him hard. All his doubts were quiet and his worries silent, at least for now.

Wilson heard the screen door on the house snap closed, and he stopped kissing. Steve looked at him, and they both began to smile, huge smiles, like they both knew they were going to get the one thing they wanted most. "After dinner," Wilson said, and Steve nodded, picked up the broom, and began sweeping again. Wilson knew he needed to find something to do or else he'd probably end up doing something in the barn that he should be doing with Steve in a proper bed.

"Dinner will be ready in an hour," Maria said from the barn door. "Is everything okay? It looks like a house exploded out here."

"It seems to be," Wilson said.

"Good. The power is back and so are the phones. Mr. Dakota called and he said they were fine too. He's still trying to figure out where all this came from to make sure no one was hurt."

"Thanks, Maria," Wilson said, and she stepped forward, looking at Steve working inside the barn and then at him.

"You deserve to be happy, Señor Wilson," Maria said, and then she turned to walk back toward the house. Wilson watched her go, thanking his lucky stars that he'd asked her to come here. His gaze traveled back to the barn, and he watched as the doors opened and Steve strode out in the paddocks, bending over to pick up the bits of fluff. Once he had the one paddock clear, he led Lilly out of the barn. She seemed happy to be back outside, and she showed it by butting his chest with her head. Steve had a way with horses, there was no doubt about that, and Wilson was beginning to realize that he had a way with his heart too.

Without thinking, Wilson found himself walking toward his bedroom. Hand on his guitar, he found his way back to the porch, watching as Steve worked with the horses. Before he realized it, Wilson's guitar was on his knee and his fingers strummed the strings. Music flowed through his mind as he watched Steve lead Chester out of the barn, the large horse prancing happily. The air smelled as fresh and clean as Wilson had ever known, the evening light shining off the glistening grass.

Lines of music filled his mind, flowing directly to his hands as he strummed the guitar. "Shining grass, tight cowboy ass," Wilson sang. He often worked in a stream of consciousness, so sometimes he got silly nonsense. "Walking away from me." Wilson liked the way that sounded. "Walking away from me," he sang again and again as the music began to play in his head. "Walking away, walking away, long legs walking away from me." Wilson smiled as the refrain played in his mind. It sounded perfect, and he continued playing. "I watch you every day, taking care of all I see, but the one thing I want most, can it ever be? Do you love me, do you need me, is it destiny? Or am I meant to only ever see, your long legs walking away from me? Walking away, walking away, walking away from me."

Wilson sang it a few times and then tried adding more. Tunes played out, and eventually Wilson's mind settled on one, and he sang the verse and refrain together. A hand settled on his shoulder, and he looked at Maria standing next to him. "Dinner is ready, Señor Wilson." He nodded and blinked. The sun was gone, and darkness was falling around him. "I didn't want to disturb you."

"Thank you, I'll be right in," he said, listening for the song he'd been working on. Sometimes they came to him and then disappeared again, but this one seemed to be staying. Standing up, Wilson followed Maria inside, and after setting his guitar on a chair, he joined the others, already eating, at the table. Wilson wasn't in the mood for talking at all; he was too deep inside his head. The others talked, and the conversation went all around him with none of it registering as his song began to play once again. He ate automatically, and once the hunger was satisfied, left the table. After retrieving his guitar, Wilson went to his room and found a music pad. At the small desk he'd always used, Wilson sat down and wrote out his song. The verses came together, and by the time he looked up from his work, the windows were dark, as was the rest of the room, with only a ring of light from the small lamp he was working by.

Wilson barely registered that someone had opened his door, and only when Steve actually walked into the room did the musical haze that had engulfed him finally lift enough for him to be aware of what was happening around him. "Are you always like that?" Steve asked, and Wilson blinked, forcing himself to comprehend the words.

"I think so. When I really feel the music, it tends to take over everything," Wilson explained, standing up on legs that felt a bit wobbly.

"I heard you as you sang," Steve told him in a whisper as he came closer. "Did you write that because of me?"

Wilson nodded. He wasn't going to lie. He'd been watching Steve when everything fell into place. Steve stepped away, and Wilson saw Steve's Wrangler-encased butt swing slightly as he moved across the room. The bedroom door closed with a click, and Steve turned to face him, eyes wide and shining in the low light. Wilson blinked a few times, thinking this was a mirage his music-rattled brain was serving up for him, but the kiss wasn't his imagination, or the heat in his blood. Steve sucked on his lips, the kisses intense and almost brutal. Wilson wrapped his arms around Steve's waist, tilting his head up for more kisses, which had softened in feel but ramped up in their intense need.

Steve lifted Wilson out of the chair, or had he simply gone willingly? Wilson didn't know or care as Steve led him to the bed. Steve removed his shirt, dropping it on the floor before pulling Wilson's up over his head. Once it joined Steve's, the kisses resumed, so deep Wilson could feel them in his toes.

"God, Steve," Wilson murmured before he began to fall back onto the bed. Once he stopped bouncing, Steve climbed on top of him. Straddling Wilson's waist, he roamed his hands over his chest. Wilson's eyes had fallen closed, but the hesitation in Steve's touch had them sliding open. He was greeted by beautiful blue eyes filled with insecurity. "What is it?"

"I've never done this before," Steve said, glancing away. Wilson reached up and stroked Steve's face as relief washed through him. Wilson knew Steve had done things to survive, and he was happy he hadn't.... "I'm not really sure what I should do."

"Whatever you want. Do whatever you always dreamed you could do when you were alone in bed."

Steve smiled and leaned forward, running his tongue along Wilson's chest. "I love that you're a little hairy," Steve told him before his tongue circled one of his nipples. Wilson arched under the sensation, trying to show Steve what he was doing to him without startling his young lover. "Am I doing this right?"

Wilson gently took Steve's hands in his, bringing him forward until their lips met. "You can't do anything wrong, I promise." As they kissed, Wilson shifted them on the bed, repositioning Steve until his head rested on the pillows, letting his hands feast on golden spot-tanned skin. It was obvious that Steve worked outside: wherever the sun kissed, he was golden, and where his skin had been hidden, Steve was almost as white as milk. Wilson lightly nipped at Steve's neck, listening for those tiny moans that told him what Steve liked. Wilson heard them, soft and long, coming from deep in Steve's chest.

"Is this okay?" Wilson asked, dipping his head to lick one of Steve's nipples, finding out quickly that they were exceedingly sensitive, if Steve's reaction was any indication. Steve whimpered, and Wilson caught glimpses of him biting his lower lip. "Let it go. You can make as much noise as you want." Wilson sucked on a perky bud, and Steve began to cry out softly.

"Willie," Steve cried, and Wilson paused, taking in the blissful look in his lover's eyes. For a second, he thought Steve was doing what others had done, calling for Willie Meadows during sex, but Steve wasn't. "Please."

Wilson released the nipple from between his lips, kissing his way down Steve's flat stomach, licking and tasting hot, luscious skin. A light trail of hair led from Steve's belly button to the top of his pants, and Wilson followed it down, opening his belt and parting the fabric of his jeans as he followed the light trail further and further. "Has anyone ever?" Wilson nuzzled Steve's bulge through the cotton of his briefs, and Steve bucked into the sensation, making small needy cries. "I'll take that as a no." Wilson chuckled, and he felt Steve shiver under him and then still.

"I can't do this," Steve said softly, and Wilson stopped. "I thought I could, but it isn't fair to you. When I was on the road trying to get here...." Steve began pulling away from him, and Wilson watched as Steve pulled his legs to his chest, curling into a tight ball. "I didn't think it would matter, but it does."

"I know you had to do things you aren't proud of. Remember, you offered to do those things for me? You were trying to survive." Wilson shifted on the bed, sitting next to Steve, holding him.

"I didn't think it would matter. The past was the past and all that, but it does," Steve told him in a broken voice.

"No, it doesn't. I'm not with you the way they were, and I won't be. I care about you, and that's why I'm here. I hope you care for me too." Wilson was beginning to realize just how innocent Steve really was, and that the bravado and flirting were only a cover. "You don't owe me an explanation for your past. All you need to worry about is right now. The past can't be changed by any of us, no matter how much we wish we could." There were things Wilson wished he could change in his past, like Clay, but he'd learned from that experience.

"It doesn't bother you?" Steve asked quietly.

"Of course it does. That people would do that to another person in exchange for helping them is atrocious, and if I could get my hands on them, I'd wring their necks. So, yes, it does matter, but not in the way you're thinking it does. You were very innocent before all this began with your father, and you learned that the world can be harsh. We all learn that at one time or another. And unfortunately you learned it when there was no one around to watch your back." Wilson touched Steve's chin, tilting his head before kissing his lips. When Steve didn't respond, he did it again, and this time Steve parted his lips for him. Wilson felt Steve uncurl beneath him, and he threaded his arms loosely around Wilson's neck.

Wilson loved the way Steve responded to him, but rather than pick up where they left off, Wilson soothed and petted, trying to show Steve that being with someone you cared about was different from what he'd done on the road. Wilson shifted on the bed, straddling Steve's hips once he'd stretched out. "I want you to lay back and let me show you how great being loved can be," Wilson purred in his deep voice, and Steve nodded slightly, his eyes widening when once again Wilson licked one of his pebbly buds. Just like before, Steve reacted, but this time he thrust his chest forward, and Wilson gave him more as his thumb and forefinger plucked at the other. The soft sounds Steve made filled the room with moans and whimpers that went right to Wilson's cock. He wanted Steve so badly he could barely think straight, but the need to take his time for Steve kept him in check.

Kissing his way down Steve's belly, Wilson began to hum the tune that had been running through his head. As he nuzzled Steve's cock through the cotton, the humming in his head increased, turning into the words of the song he'd just written. Steve's moans were like an accompaniment, and as he peeled down the fabric, they fell into harmony. Steve's cock bounced against his stomach, and as Wilson stroked the thick length, the accompaniment became the melody as the tune in his head retreated, taking background to the music Steve was making. He tapped Steve's hips and tugged down his pants, and Steve kicked them off. Wilson grinned wickedly before licking his way up the shaft. When his tongue passed over the head, Steve's flavor burst on his tongue, and he took the head between his lips, sucking harder as Steve slipped into his mouth.

"Willie!" Steve cried and began to buck. Wilson placed his hand on his lover's hips, gentling him back onto the bed. Steve panted hard and complied as Wilson took him to the root.

Wilson sucked and bobbed his head, loving the way Steve felt as he slid across his tongue, listening to the needy sounds Steve made when he teased the underside with the tip of his tongue. Lifting his eyes, he could see Steve's lips trembling, his hands balled into fists that gripped the bedding. He could tell Steve wasn't going to last much longer, and that was fine. Wilson wanted to blow Steve's mind, so he slipped a finger next to Steve's cock, getting it good and wet before sliding it between Steve's legs, teasing his opening before slipping the finger inside the tightest heat he'd ever felt in his life. Wilson's cock jumped and throbbed in his pants, and he nearly came right there when Steve howled. And when Wilson found that spot, Steve seemed to lose it, bucking and panting as he came hard and fast down Wilson's throat.

Steve collapsed back on the bed, and Wilson continued sucking for a few seconds before letting Steve's cock slip from his mouth. As he brought their lips together, Wilson heard Steve moan slightly. "What's that?" Steve asked, licking his lips.

"That's you," Wilson answered with a wink before kissing him again.

"What about you?" Steve asked, squirming on the bed to get out from under him before pressing Wilson back on the mattress. "I want to do the same to you." Steve was already opening Wilson's pants, and there was no way he was going to argue. He'd imagined Steve's lips around him so many times that the chance to feel the real thing made him jittery. Steve tugged off his pants, throwing them to the floor with a flourish before tugging down his boxers. They joined the pile, or more accurately, landed somewhere on the dresser, but Wilson didn't care—Steve was licking and sucking every bit of skin he could get his lips on. It was like Steve didn't know where to settle and wanted everything all at once.

"I'm not going anywhere, sweetheart, so you've got all the time in the world." Wilson lay back on the bedding, and Steve curled next to him, all hands, lips, and tongue. Wilson's nipples were laved and sucked, and his skin caressed in ways that made him quiver. Steve certainly seemed to have a knack for giving pleasure. When Steve's kisses trailed down his stomach, Wilson felt his cock throb with every touch, but Steve never touched him there. Instead, he trailed his lips and hands down one of his legs before traveling up the other. Every time Steve got close to his dick, Wilson would go stock still, willing Steve to take him, do something to give him relief. "You're such a tease," Wilson said through gritted teeth.

"I don't mean to be," Steve said softly, and Wilson caressed Steve's cheek as he once again went for one of his nipples, sucking hard enough that Wilson thought he might have a mark, not that he minded in the least. Wilson had wanted this so badly ever since he'd first seen Steve, so as long as Steve was doing the touching, Wilson was a happy man.

To Wilson's relief and pleasure, Steve finally curled his fingers around his cock. Wilson nearly jumped out of his skin, the touch was now so unexpected. Steve's strokes were slow but firm, and Wilson watched his younger lover with rapt attention, doing everything he could not to beg for release. When Steve's lips tentatively joined his hand, Wilson was in heaven. It didn't matter that Steve was tentative. Wilson had not expected Steve to want to take him orally after what it sounded like he'd gone through to get here. But the more Steve tried, the more confident he seemed to get, and soon Wilson was writhing on the bed, balancing on the knife edge of passion. Steve pulled his mouth away, stroking quickly, and Wilson tumbled over the abyss, coming hard onto his stomach.

Everything seemed quiet when he came down from his post-climactic high, and the first thing Wilson did was tug Steve to him. The house was quiet except for what sounded like rain on the roof, gentle this time rather than storming, like it had before. "Why don't we clean up? Have you ever showered with anyone?" Steve shook his head and smiled. "Then you're in for a treat."

Their shower ended up using most of the hot water, and by the time they climbed into bed together, they were both very relaxed. Steve seemed to fall right to sleep, but Wilson stayed awake. The house was completely quiet, and even the rain seemed to have stopped. Getting up, Wilson opened the bedroom window to let in fresh air. As he looked outside, headlights came down the road, the vehicle slowing at the driveway before continuing on. Wilson knew that eventually those headlights wouldn't continue on, and he wondered what they would do then.

A FEW nights later, Wilson woke to the sound of his phone ringing. Reaching across Steve to the table, he smiled at his sleeping lover. The man could sleep through just about anything, unless it had to do with the animals. If there was something wrong, the slightest cry seemed to have him awake almost instantly. "Hello," Wilson answered, looking at the clock.

"It's Howard. I've been trying to get in touch with you for two days. The record company loved your song, and they're wondering when you'll have the rest."

"Howard, it's four in the morning. People work here, and you could have woken the entire house." Well, he'd already woken half of it, and Steve worked hard enough that he needed his sleep.

"Like I said, I've been trying to get you for days, so I decided to try before the ass crack of dawn." Howard took a second to breathe, and Wilson left the bedroom, walking across the hall to the bathroom so he wouldn't disturb Steve. "The studio has also sent over the final contract for your debut film appearance. Your character isn't the lead, but we knew that. The script looks really good. The part is interesting, and I think you can do a great job with it. You might even steal the picture if you play it right." Howard sounded so pleased. "So how is everything in Wyoming?"

"Fine. I bought some horses, and I'm learning how to ride. This weekend we're going to a good old-fashioned ranch barbecue. Why don't you come out for a few days in a few weeks, and we can go over some business and review that script," Wilson offered. Anything to get Howard off the phone so he could go back to bed.

"I'd also like to hear the songs you're working on," Howard said.

"I sent you the one that's done. That'll have to be enough for now." The truth was, that song was the only thing he'd written or felt like writing, but he wasn't going to tell Howard that. "Good night, and I'll see you in a few weeks." Wilson hung up before Howard could protest.

Chapter Six

"RELAX AND turn Rudy to the right," Steve said from the side of the ring as Wilson sat on his horse. Wilson had had a few lessons, and he was already beginning to get the hang of riding. Of course, it helped that his horse, Rudy, was the sweetest, best-natured animal Steve had ever seen in his life. "Perfect, now walk him across the ring." They had been working on control for the last few lessons, and Wilson was coming along. "Make one more circuit and you've probably had enough for now." Steve knew that spending too much time in the saddle right away could make anyone sore, and the last thing Steve wanted was for Wilson to be sore there. Wilson made one more circuit before carefully dismounting Rudy and leading him back into the barn.

"Will we be trail riding soon?" Wilson asked as he unsaddled his horse. "Just being in the ring is a little boring."

"I know, but I want you to be able to control the horse if something happens. Once you learn control, we can trail ride all you want," Steve answered with a smile. "Maybe tomorrow we can ride back to the river near the base of the mountains. It isn't too far, and it should be a nice day." Steve moved closer, and Wilson leaned over the saddle blanket he was carrying to give him a kiss. "Is something wrong?" Steve asked after the unusually chaste kiss.

"Not with you, but I think the people looking for you are back." Wilson hung the blanket in the tack room to dry.

"I've seen them too," Steve admitted. "I'd hoped they were gone for good. I've only seen the truck come by the ranch once, but I caught a glimpse of them the last time I was in town. I don't know for sure it was them, and I'm not sure they saw me, but...."

Steve wasn't sure what to think, but he hated the thought of what they wanted and what would happen if they found him alone.

"What do you want to do?" Wilson looked very concerned, and Steve didn't doubt that for the first time he actually had someone who would be there for him.

"Before, you said to stop hiding, and I've done that. I'm wondering if we shouldn't confront them. Maybe see if we can get some friends to help. I wonder if a show of force will get them to leave me alone." Steve was getting tired of being scared all the time, and he was tired of hiding. Maybe his dad's minions would leave if they knew he had friends and was willing to put up a fight.

"If that's what you want to do, I'll be there with you," Wilson said, and Steve felt a chill slide up his spine.

"You can't. You're famous, and Dad will use that against you. If he gets wind that you're with me, he'll spread it to the world that you're gay. Even if we weren't seeing each other that way, you'd be guilty by association." Steve moved closer to Wilson so he could look into his soft eyes. "I know you want to help, and I appreciate it more than you can ever know, but I won't allow my father or his bigotry to hurt you." His heart ached at the thought that he or his past would hurt Wilson. Wilson had been good to Steve, and he didn't want to repay Wilson with trouble. For the first time since he'd known him, Steve saw a touch of fear in Wilson's eyes. Steve knew as well as Wilson that those kinds of rumors by themselves would be enough to hurt his career, let alone facts with proof. He knew entertainers, some quite famous, had been coming out of the closet for years, but not in the machismo world of Western and cowboy music.

"I'm not going to let you face them alone." The fear in Wilson's eyes was still there, but it was joined by steely determination.

"Okay." Steve smiled with relief. "But you have to promise to let me fight my own battle. I've come to realize that I'll never be rid of any of them unless I stand up for myself. You told me to stop hiding, and that was the right thing, but it's only half the battle," Steve explained with more confidence than he felt. Wilson nodded, but somewhat reluctantly. Steve knew he was right, but saying and doing were two different things. And the thought of approaching the men his father had sent to bring him back made his stomach tie in knots, but things could not continue as they were, not if he wanted to stay on the ranch— something Steve wanted more than he'd ever wanted anything in his life. The ranch didn't simply feel like a home; it made him truly happy.

"You don't have to stand up to them right now, because we should be getting ready for the party," Wilson reminded him, and they walked toward the barn door. "Dakota said to arrive about two and that dinner would be ready about six." Wilson wandered to the paddock, where Hunter, the expensive horse that Wilson had bought at auction, was munching on grass. "Will you leave the horses in their paddocks?" Wilson always asked Steve for his judgment whenever it came to the horses, and it felt good to be trusted like that. Steve's father rarely trusted anyone, but Wilson was very different from his father in so many ways.

"Most of them," Steve explained. "But I'll move Hunter into his stall just before we leave. I found out the hard way that if he gets a good running start, he can jump a fence higher than that." Steve looked at Wilson with a grin. "While we're at the party, I'm hoping to talk to some people about possibly training him as a jumper. He has speed and amazing height. He could be a great hunter, but that sort of training is a bit out of my expertise."

"Whatever you think is best," Wilson told him with a slight shoulder nudge. "I trust you to know what you're doing." Wilson smiled at him, and Steve felt warm inside. After watching the horse for a few more minutes, they both headed into the quiet house. Wilson started the shower, and Steve joined him, pushing aside the curtain and stepping behind his naked lover. Steve wrapped his arms around Wilson's waist, chest pressed to his back, cock nestling between Wilson's cheeks. He loved the feel of Wilson's skin as they slid against one another. Steve groaned as Wilson pressed back against him.

"Fuck me, Steve," Wilson groaned, his hands pressed to the tile to steady himself.

Steve wanted to very badly, and his cock throbbed in its confines between them. But they hadn't done that yet, and he wasn't quite sure he was up for that, even though his body seemed more than ready.

"I really want to feel you," Wilson said as he turned his head, and they kissed. It was sloppy and got more so as Wilson ground his butt on Steve's cock, making Steve's vision blur.

"How about tonight when I get you home?" Steve asked as Wilson continued moving his cheeks up and down Steve's shaft. Steve began thrusting his hips as he slid his hand down to Wilson's groin, stroking his cock as the water cascaded around them. "Does that feel good?" Steve whispered in Wilson's ear before sucking on it.

"Fuck yes," Wilson groaned as he thrust into Steve's hand, and Steve tightened his grip, running his thumb over the head on Wilson's next thrust. They continued moving together, filling the bathroom with groans of pleasure. Steve would never tire of those sounds Wilson made. He knew when he was happy, because he would hum softly. But as his desire built, the hums would turn to deep, throaty moans that drove Steve wild, because when he heard those, he knew Wilson was reaching the heights of pleasure.

"I want you to come with me," Steve moaned as he kissed Wilson's shoulder, his climax building, balls already tightening to his body. Steve stoked harder, Wilson's cock throbbing in his hand, their thrusting becoming ragged as they both neared their peak. Steve felt Wilson's dick throb and heard him cry out as release overtook his lover, and Steve followed right behind, thrusting against Wilson's butt. His climax barreled into him, and Steve clung to Wilson as he came hard between their bodies, his release painting Wilson's skin before the water washed it away.

Steve rested his head on Wilson's shoulder as he caught his breath. He felt Wilson turn, and then he was being held and hugged, kisses peppering his neck. "You're amazing," Wilson whispered into his ear, and Steve would have laughed if Wilson hadn't moved them directly beneath the spray. They spent some time washing and playing together before turning off the water.

"If you keep looking at me like that, we'll never make it to the party," Steve told Wilson, who stood in his doorway watching him pull on his clothes. Wilson growled, and Steve laughed, buttoning up his pants. After pulling on his shirt, Steve sat on the edge of the bed, tugging on his boots as Wilson continued watching him. He picked up his dirty shirt from the floor and tossed it at Wilson, who dodged out of the way.

"What was that for?" he asked indignantly, tossing it back.

"If you don't stop giving me those bedroom looks, I'll rip your clothes off, and we'll never make the party. And your neighbors and friends will think you blew them off." Steve set his booted foot on the floor as Wilson rushed him. Steve sprawled on the bed, laughing as he bounced.

"I'll definitely blow something," Wilson drawled into his ear, and Steve's jeans went two sizes too tight. Wilson sucked on his ear, and Steve moaned, already clutching at Wilson's clothes. His jeans parted, and Wilson yanked them down his legs. Before Steve could say anything, his brains were being sucked out through his dick even as the air whooshed from his lungs.

"Willie," Steve gasped as Wilson's head bobbed on his cock, doing that thing with his tongue that drove him completely wild. He'd come in the shower fifteen minutes earlier, and already his balls were tightening and his breath coming in pants. Clamping his eyes closed, he felt his climax begin to build, and before he knew it, Wilson had sucked him to a breathtaking orgasm that left him flopped on the bed and unable to move.

Steve knew he must look totally debauched, and looking down only confirmed it. His pants were around his ankles, shirt still on, dick hanging out, and he didn't care in the least. Steve saw the self-satisfied look on Wilson's face as he licked his lips.

"Are you ready to go now?" Wilson asked him with a crook of his eyebrows. Steve wasn't ready to move, but the front door opened, and he heard Alicia's excited voice asking if she could ride her pony to the party. Steve hurriedly pulled up his pants and was just fastening his belt when Alicia rushed into the room, throwing herself at him.

Steve caught her and twirled her into the air. "They'll have their own horses at the party, and I suspect there will be someone willing to give you a ride." Her cry was deafening, and Steve carried her into the living room, where Maria waited for all of them. Wilson escorted them all out the door, and just before they left, Steve moved Hunter into the barn.

The cab of the truck filled with excitement as they rode the few miles to Dakota and Wally's house. The yard was filled with mostly trucks, and Alicia held onto her mother as they got out and the sounds of almost a hundred voices swept over them.

"I'm glad you could come." Wally greeted them with a huge smile and led them to where the party was in full swing along the side of the house. Music had been set up, and kids were playing games on the front lawn.

"Why isn't the party in back?" Wilson asked, and Steve's eyes widened.

"You haven't been here before, have you?" Steve smirked and turned to Wally. "Is it okay if I show him and Alicia the kitties?"

Wally grinned. "I'll take you back in just a minute." Wally hurried away and went into the house, returning with a covered metal container. "It's about feeding time."

Steve saw the surprise on Wilson's face as Wally led them around the back of the house and across the yard to an area under the trees. A roar sounded as they approached, and Alicia jumped back and tried to climb him. He picked her up, and they approached slowly. "Ay dios mio," Maria said under her breath as they approached the cages.

"This is Shahrazad," Wally said as he pointed toward the impressive prowling tiger. "She can be protective of her den, so stay clear." Wally approached carefully and placed what looked like raw meat in a chute, and it fell into the cage. The tiger immediately pounced on it.

"This is Manny. He's less aggressive as long as he gets fed." Wally placed his food in a chute as well. "I used to have a lion that loved to get his belly scratched. Whenever he saw me, he'd roll over and purr louder than an airplane."

"What happened to him?" Alicia asked in a small voice, hands staying close to her body.

"He died. Most of these animals are old. I try to find good homes for all of them if I can, but some stay here to live out the rest of their lives. Shahrazad is being shipped to a zoo next week. It took me awhile, but I found one that was willing to take her because she's young and extremely rare. So she'll move on, and another animal will take her place."

"Why do you keep them here?" Wilson asked, keeping his distance but clearly fascinated.

"Most would be euthanized if I didn't. People try to keep them as pets and find out they can't. Circuses donate them if they're uncontrollable or get too old to perform. Shahrazad attacked a trainer at a circus, and she was completely uncontrollable. So I agreed to take her." Wally continued talking as he fed the animals. "She's a Bengal tiger, which are extremely endangered and rare, so the zoo is hoping to use her for breeding. I hope this goes through. I've had a number of other deals with her fall through because she's such a handful." Wally glared at the tiger, who looked up from her food and tilted her head like she knew Wally was talking about her. She yowled and then went back to eating.

"What are those over there?" Alicia pointed to more pens a ways away from the others.

"I sometimes get other exotic animals that need homes, and those are pens for them. I deal mainly with cats now, but I don't like to turn animals away if I can help them."

Steve saw Wilson look all around him. "How do you pay for all this?"

"Circuses often make a donation to help with the care, but mostly I pay for it. The grocery store in town saves bones and scraps for me, which they sell at a very reasonable price." Wally motioned back toward the house, and they all began to walk toward the party. "Dakota thought I was crazy to begin with, but in most ways the shelter pays for itself. Shahrazad isn't being sent to that zoo for free. She's a very expensive animal, and what they are paying me will allow the shelter to run for a year. All I want to do is break even on food, supplies, and the cost of care. Anything above that, I use to try to expand the facilities."

They approached the party, and Steve set Alicia on her feet. The other children seemed to gravitate toward her, and Steve saw Maria watching as her little girl ran off to play. Maria moved toward a group of women, and he smiled when they folded her into their group. Steve kept wanting to reach out and touch Wilson, but he knew that was something he probably shouldn't do in public, not when half the people at the party recognized Wilson.

"Willie Meadows," a large man called as he made his way over while they were at the drink area getting a couple of beers. "I'm Harold Thompson, mayor of our fair town, and it's an honor to have you living in our community. I trust we can count on you for plenty of civic support." The man oozed "politician," and Steve watched Wilson, wondering what he'd do.

"Well, Harold, out here I'm just plain Wilson. And of course I plan to do my civic duty, but mostly I'm here to run my ranch and enjoy the peace and quiet. I have to leave to do a movie in a few months, and then a concert tour in about a year. I want this to be a place of refuge and peace, where people respect my privacy." Wilson took a drink from his beer, and Steve saw the mayor's face fall just a little.

"Harold," a frail-sounding voice called. Steve turned, seeing Dakota pushing a man in a wheelchair. He was tilted back to a slightly reclining position and covered with a blanket even on a warm day. "Leave the man alone. He doesn't need to serve on one of your ridiculous committees. What are you working on now, the committee to spread manure?"

"Dad," Dakota said, and the mayor found someone else to talk to.

"The only reason that man got elected mayor is because no one else wanted the job," Dakota's dad added.

"Wilson, I'd like you to meet my father, Jefferson," Dakota said, and Steve saw Wilson reach out and shake the wheelchair-bound man's curled hand.

"It's a pleasure to meet you, Mr. Meadows," Jefferson said with a half smile.

"Please call me Wilson, and the pleasure is all mine." Wilson leaned a little closer. "Thank you for getting rid of the mayor. Never could stand politicians," he said with a wink, and Jefferson nodded slightly in return. "This is Steve. He's training horses for me." Steve shook the man's hand the way Wilson had. Jefferson seemed so fragile, and yet there was a strength in him that surprised Steve. His eyes were bright, and it was obvious there was intelligence and spirit inside the twisted body.

Steve felt surprisingly disappointed at the way Wilson had introduced him, but he tried to keep his smile in place. Rationally, he knew that he was more to Wilson than just the guy that trained and took care of his horses, and that Wilson was simply being cautious, but it still hurt. After excusing himself, Steve wandered away to where some of the men were pitching horseshoes, and he watched them for a while, but his eyes kept wandering to where Wilson stood talking with a group of people clustered around him like he was holding court. Steve sighed to himself and tried to watch the game, but it didn't interest him.

"Everything okay?" Steve turned around and saw Haven standing just behind him.

"I guess." Steve took a drink from his beer to cover his distraction as he once again snuck a peek at his lover. "I'm just being silly." He was; he knew that. Wilson cared about him, or at least Steve thought he did.

"Would you like to go for a ride? We've got the horses saddled, and some of us are going to give the younger children a chance to spend some time on a horse. You can join us if you like, there's room."

Steve finished the last of his beer. "I'd like that, and so would Alicia."

"Good," Haven said, and he led Steve over where the saddled horses were waiting, with a number of kids milling around waiting for a chance, Alicia among them. When she saw Steve, Alicia hurried over.

"I get to ride a real horse," she said as Steve lifted her off her feet.

"Yes. You and I are going to ride together," Steve told her, and she giggled as Steve put her down. "You need to tell your mother where you'll be so she doesn't worry."

Alicia raced across the yard to Maria, and Steve saw them talking for a minute, and then Alicia ran back with a huge grin on her face. "Mama said it was okay," Alicia said happily, her hands behind her back, her little body rocking with excitement.

"This lady will work for you," Haven told him as he indicated the chestnut mare waiting patiently at one of the fences. Steve climbed into the saddle, and then Haven handed Alicia up to him. Steve moved back, settling Alicia in front of him. She vibrated with energy, she was so excited, as she leaned forward to pat the horse's neck with her small hands.

"You a nice horsey," she said over and over as she continued rubbing the mare's neck. "What's her name?" Alicia asked, looking back at Steve. Thankfully, Haven was nearby.

"Her name's Lulu," Haven said with a grin as he too mounted one of the horses and one of the young boys was passed up to him. "Is everybody ready?" There were four horses and eight riders in their group, and Haven led them out of the yard and down along a trail. "We'll ride to the river and back. That shouldn't be too long."

Steve looked back toward the gathered group, and he saw Wilson still in the center of his group. Steve wanted to wave, but it didn't look as though Wilson even realized he was gone. Alicia talked and talked, commenting on everything from the trees to the heat, from the sun to the way the horse walked. Steve kept an eye out and answered all Alicia's questions as best he could, but his mind seemed to wander back to Wilson. Maybe he was simply fooling himself to believe that a famous man like Wilson could really care for a guy like him. Steve didn't have anything to offer him, not really. Besides, Wilson would be around other famous and beautiful people when he was filming that movie, and he could have anyone he wanted while he was on tour.

"Don't be sad," Alicia said as she turned to peer up at him. Steve smiled at her, and she seemed satisfied. As they approached the river, Alicia wanted to get down, and Steve could hear the other kids asking too, but they continued on. Steve knew the parents would not appreciate their returning wet children to them. Not to mention there were few things worse than a wet, squishy saddle. As they rode along the sparkling water, the breeze cooled slightly in the shade of the large trees that lined the banks. "Can we have a picnic here sometime?" Alicia asked as her head turned to look at the canopy of leaves above them. "I've never seen trees like this before. Where do they keep the palm trees?"

Steve chuckled softly. "There aren't any palm trees here. It gets too cold in the winter. So there are different kinds of trees. See," Steve said, pointing "these trees lose their leaves in the winter, so all you see are the branches. But before they do, Mother Nature paints the leaves all kinds of different colors. It's really pretty." Steve used the explanation his mother had told him when he was young, and Alicia seemed fascinated.

"Who's Mother Nature? Can we visit her and tell her to paint the leaves now? I want to see the colors," Alicia said in that way kids have that makes the impossible seem totally reasonable.

"Mother Nature takes care of all the animals and plants. She's very busy, and we need to let her do things in her own time. It'll get colder soon enough, and then the leaves will change. You won't miss it, I promise." Steve smiled, and Alicia went on to talk about something else as they made the turn back toward the ranch. When they arrived, Steve handed Alicia down to Dakota, and she ran toward her mother before skidding to a stop.

"Thank you, Uncle Steve," she called before running excitedly to her mother. Steve saw a boy about six standing near his horse, and Dakota handed him up.

"I'm Steve, what's your name?" Steve asked the youngster.

"I'm Carl," he answered, patting Lulu's neck the same way Alicia had.

"How old are you?" Steve asked as they waited for the others to get ready. Steve glanced toward the gathering, and it was instantly apparent where Wilson was because of the crowd around him.

"I'm five," he said, holding up a full hand of fingers, flashing Steve a huge smile. "Did you come with Willie Meadows?"

"Yes. I take care of his horses," Steve said with a touch of sarcasm that of course went over Carl's head.

"My mother thinks he's dreamy. She said she heard he was going to be here. She said she was going to try to bag him, but I don't know what that means." Carl gave him a funny look, but Steve kept his face bland. He wished her luck. The other riders were ready, and they began their slow walk, following the same trail as they had before. The kids seemed to have a great time, but Steve kept his attention on where they were going as his thoughts swirled around Wilson and what was actually happening between them. When they got back, Steve handed Carl down and then slid off the horse himself. He helped Haven unsaddle them before releasing the horses into their paddocks. Steve then wandered back to the party. He didn't approach the group of people around Wilson, instead walking to the drink area. He definitely needed a beer or six. Sipping from his bottle, he glanced over at the crowd and caught a glimpse of Wilson. He had a smile on his face, but it looked forced. Their eyes met for a second before a thin blonde with big hair stepped in the way. He saw Carl approach her, and Steve shook his head to himself. If she wanted to try to bag Wilson, she at least had ammunition—too bad it was the wrong caliber.

People filtered around him. He didn't know them, and they barely seemed to acknowledge him. Taking another swig from his beer, Steve glanced in Wilson's direction once again. This was becoming ridiculous, and Steve knew it, but he couldn't take his eyes off Wilson for very long. He longed to touch him, hold him, and push all the hangers-on away. He saw Carl's mother throw her head back and laugh at something, hair flouncing, like some deranged trollop. The men were still playing horseshoes, and the *clink clink* of metal on metal sounded in the distance. Steve was thinking of finding someone to talk with when he saw the group part and Wilson's eyes met his. Steve saw the plastered smile once again, and even from this distance he could see the tired lines and the dull look in his eyes. When Steve returned his gaze, Wilson's smile brightened slightly. He nodded to the people around him before walking toward Steve.

Steve smiled, but then let it fade. He didn't need to advertise how happy he was looking at his lover. Reaching into the cooler, Steve pulled out a bottle and opened it, handing it to Wilson.

"God, I need this," Wilson said before gulping from the bottle. "It's almost as bad as a personal appearance in LA, except they're more aggressive, if that's possible." Wilson looked back at the group. "That blonde bombshell actually grabbed my butt." Steve growled and tried to cover it by taking a drink, but it didn't work. "That woman is aggressive as hell."

"I gave her son a ride, and he informed me that his mother wanted to 'bag' you." Steve tried to keep from laughing, but couldn't.

"There's only one person I want to bag me, and he'll get to do that after we get home." Wilson winked, and Steve smirked before looking away, covering his expression with a pull on his bottle.

"There you are." The buxom blonde who could only be Carl's mother out to bag herself a man flounced up to Wilson, taking his arm in hers. "I would just love to cook for you," she said breathily, and Steve rolled his eyes behind her back, moving away from the table.

"That would be very nice, but I'm not available for quite a while. I have a great deal of work to do," Wilson explained gently, but the blonde was having none of it, sticking out her chest so Wilson knew exactly what was on offer.

"Cheryl, I believe Carl needs you. He's over by the barn," Wally said as he approached, and Steve saw her hesitate before reluctantly releasing Wilson's arm, walking away with a swing to her hips, mile-high heels leaving a trail of holes as she went. "That woman is a menace," Wally said softly. "The only reason we invite her is because Carl gets such a kick out of the horses, and I can't see punishing him because his mother is a slut." Wally glared at her retreating backside and shivered. "She actually went after Dakota last year. She and I had a little talk, and I explained to her that if she didn't leave my man alone, I'd use one of her stilettos to poke her eyes out." Wally continued glaring before bursting into a smile. "You know, after that, she proved it *is* possible to run in heels."

Steve saw Cheryl making her way back in their direction. "It looks like the horseshoes are free, let's go play."

"I don't know how," Wilson said, but Wally was unperturbed.

"It's either that or spend the next hour with Cheryl," Wally warned.

"I'll learn," Wilson said, and they made their way to the pitch. Steve had never played horseshoes either. His father didn't approve of such games. Hell, he was finding after being out of the community for a relatively short time that there were a lot of things his father didn't approve of. Wally explained the rules, and Steve saw that Cheryl made her way over and watched them play for a while, but eventually lost interest. Neither he nor Wilson was any good, but they had fun playing with some of the other men, who were helpful.

The afternoon wore on, and eventually everyone was called to dinner. Dakota's father sat at the head of one of the tables, and he and Wilson joined him, effectively shutting Cheryl out. "Don't be surprised if she shows up at your house," Dakota said as he sat across from them. "The woman's a pain."

Steve snickered. "Wally told us."

"She's also a huge gossip and a busybody, so be careful, if you know what I mean," Dakota warned. Thankfully, the conversation turned to something more pleasant.

"Would you sing a song later?" Jefferson asked softly from the head of the table, and Steve saw Wilson hesitate before agreeing. He knew Wilson really wanted to try to be a regular person, he'd said it often enough, but at a gathering like this, Willie Meadows was going to be forced to make an appearance.

"I don't have my guitar, though," Wilson explained, and Steve nudged him lightly.

"It's behind the seat in the truck. I figured you'd get roped into performing, so I put it in so you wouldn't have to go back and get it." Steve wasn't sure if Wilson would be happy with him or not. Steve heard him sigh softly before quietly telling him thank you.

Once they were done with barbecue, Dakota said a few words and then they broke out the desserts, which caused quite a stir as the kids all lined up to eat their weight in ice cream. Steve had to admit that he nearly did the same as well.

A fire was lit in a huge pit, and the adults gathered around while the kids continued playing on the lawn. Eventually, Steve saw Wilson get his guitar, and when he took his seat, silence fell, with only the crackle of the fire to break the quiet of the coming twilight.

Steve settled into a chair where he could watch Wilson without the others really realizing where he was looking. The firelight danced on Wilson's face as he placed the guitar on his knee and began strumming. Steve knew from listening that he was simply warming up and letting his mind wander. Without any explanation, Wilson broke into an old standard about the West: land, mountains, and water... cool, clear water. Wilson's voice played in Steve's mind the way it always did. He could hear the love in Wilson's voice. Steve would have liked to think that it was for him. Closing his eyes, he let the music and Wilson's voice wash over him. Steve knew everyone else around the fire heard Willie Meadows, except Steve, who heard Wilson, the man he desperately wanted to be able to think of as his.

The song ended and another began. Opening his eyes, he saw everyone around the fire entranced by his lover's voice. Steve had heard Wilson sing, both recorded and live, and he knew exactly why he was so popular. His voice felt like smooth, creamy, dark chocolate to Steve. Once you got a bite, you wanted more and more. He could see all the others around the fire slowly slipping under Wilson's spell. No one moved while Wilson sang. Hell, Steve could barely breathe, and all he wanted was more. Wilson carried out the end of the number, and then all was quiet. Steve saw people blink as they began to move and shift in their seats. Applause broke out, and Wilson said thank you before stepping away from the fire.

"Just one more," Cheryl asked as she moved closer to Wilson, tilting her head up at him. Steve could see Wilson was tired, and now he knew exactly why Wilson had moved away and bought the ranch. Everyone seemed to want a piece of him: *one more autograph, sing one more song, write one more piece of music, serve on one more committee because with you we can raise more money. Just this one thing....*

Steve stood up. He walked around the back of the ring of chairs, took the guitar from Wilson, and without a word, carried it across the dark yard to the truck. He wasn't letting anyone wring everything they could out of his lover. Wilson was a giving person; Steve had seen that firsthand, and he knew Wilson would go on and on. He opened the door, placed the guitar in its case, and then stowed it in the backseat. Steve's heart felt light. He'd seen the grateful look on Wilson's face, and he knew that was meant for only him. Closing the door, Steve was encased in near total darkness. Weaving through the darkness, he walked back toward the laughter that flowed across the range, carried on a light summer breeze.

A hand settled on his shoulder, and Steve turned, looking into familiar eyes. "We've been looking for you." Steve's heart skipped a beat, and he knew he should scream, but he couldn't. All he could do was stare.

Chapter Seven

WILSON KEPT looking to where Steve had gone, and after a minute, he got up as well. After making a detour at the drink station, he wandered over toward the truck. What he saw stopped him in his tracks. He'd know Steve anywhere just by the way he stood and moved, but he certainly didn't know the two men near him, and they appeared to be a little too close. Something told him Steve was in distress. Wilson hurried across the yard and stepped up to Steve. "What's going on?"

"These men are the ones my father sent," Steve told him, and Wilson placed his hand on Steve's back to reassure him.

"You've got two seconds before I cry out, and there will be plenty of people here who won't take too kindly to you trying to kidnap Steve." Wilson was not allowing anyone to take Steve anywhere he didn't want to go.

Both men took a step back. "Who said anything about kidnapping? We've been trying to find Steve for the last few months, ever since he escaped from the hospital."

"Then why are you here? What does my dear obsessed nutcase father want?" Steve said, and Wilson could feel the tension rolling off his lover. "Because I have no intention of going back there, ever, so you can tell my father to leave me alone." Steve stared at the men, and Wilson felt his chest fill with pride.

"Wait," one of the men said, "you think your father sent us?" He shook his head. "Not at all. We were sent by some of the other community members to make sure you were okay. They weren't happy about the way your father has been treating you and others in the community. They asked us to find you and see if you'd come back and help them throw your father out."

Wilson looked at Steve and then at both men, each of whom nodded vigorously. "I really don't care," Wilson said.

One of the men stepped closer. "You're the guy who sent us on that wild-goose chase a few weeks ago." Wilson saw him scowl and then look back at Steve. "Your father doesn't know where you are. He had Rose read your mail, but she never told him about the job offer you got. We aren't happy with the way your dad runs everyone's lives, and it wasn't fair the way he was running yours."

"Look." Wilson held up his hand. He'd had enough talking in the dark where he couldn't see anyone's face. "This is a party, and I somehow doubt you were invited. You already know where Steve lives; you've driven by enough times. So I suggest you stop by tomorrow morning, late," he added with emphasis, "and we'll talk. But we'll also have friends nearby, just in case." They nodded and backed away. Wilson watched as they walked across the yard and out to the road. Their forms retreated into the darkness, and a few minutes later he saw a truck pull out and drive away.

Wilson had no idea what to think about that encounter. "Were those the men after you? Did you recognize them?"

"Yes. I think they came to the house just after you left for LA, and I hid from them," Steve told him in a tone that sounded like a confession. "To think they were trying to find me because they were concerned about me."

Wilson wasn't buying their story, at least not totally. "When we talk to them tomorrow, we can see if their story holds water. Until then, you aren't leaving my sight. There's something rotten in Denmark, and I want to see what it is." Wilson felt a cold shiver run up his spine. What if what they said was the truth? That they wanted Steve to come back with them to help get rid of his father. What if Steve left? He'd grown up in that community, and everyone knew him there. If what these men said was true, then maybe a lot of the people didn't feel the same way Steve's father did, and maybe Steve could go home. The thought scared him, because he'd become very attached to Steve. Hell, his heart jumped every time Steve smiled, and the idea of him leaving left Wilson feeling empty. Wilson wouldn't stand in his way if Steve wanted to leave, though—he cared too much for him to do that.

"Let's find Alicia and Maria," Wilson said into the darkness, wishing he could see Steve's expression for any indication, no matter how small, of what he was thinking. "Maybe it's time to go home."

"Yeah," Steve agreed absently without turning his head to look away from where the two men's truck had disappeared. Leaving Steve alone, Wilson returned to the fire and saw that Alicia had climbed onto her mother's lap and looked to be nearly asleep. Maria looked ready to go, so he took Alicia from her arms and carried her to the truck, buckling her into the booster seat. Once everyone was in, he started driving for home.

Everyone was quiet, and Wilson simply drove. They'd all had a wonderful, but long day. During the relatively short ride, Wilson found himself looking over at Steve every few seconds, trying to get a handle on what he might be thinking, but he learned nothing.

At the ranch, he pulled close to the foreman's house. After saying good night, Maria and Alicia went inside, then he pulled into his normal parking space. Wilson didn't know what to say, and even opened his mouth to ask Steve to stay, but knew that wasn't fair. If Steve wanted to leave, him adding more pressure wouldn't help.

"I need to check on the horses," Steve said once Wilson turned off the engine. "I'll be in soon." Steve hurried to the barn, and Wilson retrieved his guitar and walked toward the house. He never made it inside. On the porch, he started to hear music floating through his mind. Sitting in one of the chairs Steve had found and refinished, Wilson placed the instrument on his knee and began to play. Unlike the last time, this tune sprang from him almost fully formed, and he recognized it as the fear and uncertainty coming to the surface. Once the tune stopped, he played it again and again, imprinting the music on his brain. Then he opened his mouth, and the words came—soft and slow, sad and scared, they came. He sang about the night, the lonely night with only the stars for company. He sang what the ranch would be like for him if Steve left, with only long, lonely nights. Wilson closed his eyes and imagined that the horses and even the crickets would be silent because of the long, lonely nights.

When the song ended, Wilson looked across the dark yard. He heard the slightest sounds coming from the barn. He always wondered how long he was gone when inspiration struck like that, though this time it seemed to have happened very quickly. Wilson unlocked the door and hurried inside. Sitting at the desk in his room, he wrote down the music and the words in a flurry of creative activity. Once he had it written down, the music usually stopped, but not this time. The long, lonely nights continued playing in Wilson's head. He dropped the music on the scanner, made a copy, and e-mailed it to Howard. The door banged closed, and Wilson looked up from where he'd been working, glancing at the clock, amazed that it had only been little over an hour since they'd arrived home.

Wilson heard Steve's footsteps come down the hall and go into his bedroom. The door closed, and Wilson turned back to his desk, staring at the song he'd written as it continued playing in his head.

A hand lightly touched his shoulder, and then lips touched his cheek just below his ear.

"You stood up for me," Steve said, and Wilson turned. Of course he'd stood up for Steve, he cared for him. Wilson swallowed. *He loved him.* In that second, Wilson knew what he was feeling. He opened his mouth to actually say the words, but Steve kissed him hard, taking possession of his mouth, and Wilson surged forward. Standing up, he guided Steve toward the bed, already pulling off his lover's shirt. His own followed rather quickly, and then they tumbled onto the bed in a tangle of legs as hands explored wantonly. Wilson felt Steve on top of him, fingers unfastening his belt, and Wilson tried to do the same. After a slight bit of energetic fumbling, the rest of their clothes joined their shirts on the floor.

They each kissed the skin they could reach as both of them writhed on the bed, greedily trying to get one more taste or caress his lover just a little more. Their erratic energy quickly turned more purposeful as lips tasted and hands explored. Sometime during their frenzied fumbling, Wilson's heart engaged, and just like that, they weren't having sex, they were making love, at least for him. Wilson wanted to think Steve felt the same way, but he couldn't be sure. And once again, he was very close to letting those three small words cross his lips, but held back. Instead, he let his body do the talking for him and hoped Steve got the message.

Wilson wasn't sure if Steve understood or not. He seemed wild and almost driven by fear. When Steve took him deep, it was like he had to have him all at once; the energy combined with the nearly feral look in his eyes drove Wilson wild as he let Steve take whatever he needed. Hell, it almost seemed to Wilson as though he were along for the ride, and what a ride it was. Wilson came in a blinding crash of light with Steve right behind him. Afterward, they settled on the bed, and Steve pressed so close Wilson could feel his heart beating and the blood rushing under his skin.

THEY DIDN'T sleep much. During the night, Steve tossed and turned, and Wilson held him. He couldn't blame his lover one single bit. He wasn't ready to fully believe the men from Steve's community, not yet, but if what they said was the truth, that could be nearly as disturbing for Steve as if they'd been trying to bring him back. And for Wilson, what they offered scared him half to death. He could fight them if they were from his father, but he couldn't fight their offer to allow him to go home.

"It's okay, I'm here," Wilson whispered into the darkness as Steve tossed once again. Scooping him into his arms, Wilson heard Steve make desperate noises and then settle once again as Wilson began stroking his arm. Eventually, Wilson fell asleep as well, waking to the sounds of Maria in the kitchen and Alicia's laughter. Steve didn't move, and Wilson carefully got out of the bed and walked quietly to the bathroom. After dressing, he left the room, closing the door without a sound.

"Is Señor Steve okay?" Maria asked when Wilson walked into the kitchen, handing him a mug of steaming coffee. Wilson nodded as he sipped tentatively, and Maria went back to her cooking.

"There are some men stopping by this morning," Wilson said tentatively, wondering how he wanted to explain things to her.

"Are these the men from last night? I see you talking to them, and Señor Steve not look happy," Maria said without looking up from the pan. The woman had the eyes of a hawk—that was the only explanation. "Alicia and I will go to our house after you eat, but you promise to call if you need us." It was only after he promised to call for help that she fixed him a plate. Steve joined them a few minutes later looking a bit "deer in the headlights" as he, too, sat down at the table. They ate in silence, with only the clink of silverware against the plates. Wilson noticed that Steve only picked at his food for a while before getting up and leaving the table, taking his mug with him as he headed out the front door. Wilson watched him go and decided Steve might need some time alone with his thoughts.

Wilson's phone rang as he finished eating. "Morning, Howard."

"This is fucking amazing!" rang through the phone. "This song you sent is incredible. I was going to say it's better than the last one, but they're both among the best you've ever written." The excitement on the other side of the line was unexpected and very gratifying. "I'll pass this on to the record company this morning. They're going to be thrilled." For a second, Howard nearly gushed. "So how are things in the sticks?"

"You've seen the music," Wilson answered, lifting his mug for another sip of coffee.

"Yeah, but I suspect it's not the wide-open spaces that are fueling this bout of creativity." There was caution and concern in Howard's voice. "I can't argue with the results, but you need to be very careful. If whatever is going on between you and that kid gets out...."

"Howard, please...."

He heard a deep breath. "Don't bullshit me, Wilson. I knew as soon as I saw that first song just whose long legs you were writing about." A huge sigh sounded as Howard trailed off. "You deserve to be happy, I know that, and goddammit, I want you to be. You deserve it. I just don't want that happiness to come at a price you aren't willing to pay." The line went quiet, and for a few seconds it seemed like Wilson was hearing his old friend. Then it was gone like a popped bubble. "So how long do you expect it to take for the rest?"

"I'll have them when I have them. The music is coming right now, and I'm going where it takes me." That was all he could ever do. Most people didn't understand that he couldn't just turn on his ability to write music. When it happened, it happened. He'd tried forcing it and always got crap, so he'd stopped, and after that always went with his inspiration. So far it hadn't steered him wrong. "I'll send you something when I have it."

"Good. I'll be out this weekend, and we can go over this script and the other deals I'm working on for you." Howard stopped talking, and Wilson waited to hear what would come next. "I know you're happy there, but I've received a number of offers. We'll review them, though, and you can tell me the ones you want to do." Was this the same Howard?

"What's with you? No pushing?"

The line stayed quiet. "I think I understand how you're feeling. Since you left town, I've had more time since I'm not babysitting you."

"Very funny, Howard," Wilson quipped lamely, but it was nice to hear happiness in Howard's voice.

"I met someone. We've been on a few dates, and she's really nice. Pretty, but down-to-earth and real." Howard sounded almost chipper.

"You deserve to be happy too, Howard, and I'll see you this weekend. Is she coming with you?"

"No. Linda has to work. So it'll be just me for a few days. I'll see you then." Howard disconnected, and Wilson set his phone on the table. After finishing his coffee, he was about to wander out to the barn, but Steve came back inside, and Wilson heard the television switch on. Maria cleaned up, and Wilson took his dishes to her before joining Steve in the living room. Maria brought in two fresh mugs of coffee before she and Alicia left the house, leaving them alone to wait.

A light knock on the door made Steve jump so fast he nearly spilled his mug, and Wilson touched his arm to reassure him before getting up to answer it. The same two men from last night stood on his porch, and in the light of day Wilson had to admit they looked a whole lot less intimidating. He wasn't sure what he'd been expecting—something out of *Men in Black*, no doubt, but not khakis and polos.

"Come on in and have a seat," Wilson said, and he sat next to Steve. Wilson wanted to take Steve and hold him close to reassure him, but not knowing what these men were after…. So he sat on the sofa and waited while Steve glared across at them without saying a word.

"I think you'd better tell us what you came here for," Wilson said, and he nearly reached out to hold Steve's hand, but held himself back once again. "So you might as well start at the beginning and make introductions."

"I'm Gilbert, and this is my brother, Jerry. We knew Steve from the community, but we didn't have much interaction together. Anyway, after Steve's father, David, sent him to that hospital, we sort of tried to keep an eye on him, but we weren't able to get in to him, and ever since he got away, we've been trying to find him," Gilbert explained before turning to Steve. "We tracked you here through the letter you got. Your father doesn't know where you are. The letter originally got delivered to Rose, and she made sure your daddy didn't see it. She then got it passed to you."

Steve nodded his agreement. "I wondered how anyone knew where I was." Steve's voice sounded flat, like he wasn't sure what to make of everything. "So what's going on and why are you here?"

Gilbert looked at Jerry and then back to Steve, who folded his arms over his chest. "We told you last night there are people in the community who aren't happy, but most of them are pretty scared of your dad."

Steve nodded slowly. "They have reason to be. I think he's starting to lose his sanity."

Jerry nodded his agreement, and Gilbert continued. "When you got away from that hospital, it gave people hope. They began talking quietly that maybe you'd come back and that it could mean the end of your father. But you stayed away. Jerry and I left to try to find you."

"What does my dad think about you leaving?" Steve asked, and Wilson could see the hard look in Steve's eyes. "Not that it particularly matters," Steve continued, without letting them answer. "What I really want to know is where were all these scared and notoriously quiet people when my father threw me in a basement room for days? What did they do then?" Steve's voice got higher, more urgent and angry.

"He's your father," Gilbert said, as though that explained everything.

Wilson's patience was beginning to wear thin. "You do realize that Steve is an adult, and no one, not even this all-mighty, all-powerful father," he said, letting sarcasm drip from his tongue, "has the right to imprison anyone against their will." What kind of people were they?

"We didn't know at first what had happened. David kept everything a secret, telling us Steve was sick. And in David's opinion, being gay is an illness. We didn't find out about the locked room and Steve being sent away until almost a week after he was gone." Gilbert swallowed hard and looked at Steve imploringly. "We honestly didn't know."

Steve didn't relax his stance one bit. "What happened to Kyle?"

"His family left in the middle of the night. Heather saw them packing things really quietly, and since she heard about what happened, she thought they were ashamed at first, but we—" Gilbert looked to Jerry for support, and he smiled slightly. "We think they left to get out from under your dad's thumb. I don't know where they went, but they're gone. We all used to believe the same thing, helping one another, living a good, clean, Christian life, brotherhood and sisterhood. It seems simple, but that's how we all wanted to live, and things have gone so very wrong." Gilbert looked worn out, like his world had come crashing down around him. "We hadn't even realized how bad it had gotten until we heard what happened to you."

"Will you help us?" Jerry pleaded, leaning forward in his chair. "That's why we wanted so desperately to find you. We need your help."

Wilson found his gaze traveling from the two men to Steve and back to them, and in a moment of clarity, he saw Gilbert and Jerry for what they were—sheep. They would follow Steve for weeks and over a thousand miles because they needed someone to lead them. Where, Wilson had no idea, and he doubted Gilbert and Jerry did, either. Steve said nothing and seemed to be lost in his own thoughts.

"It seems to me that expecting someone to solve your problems for you is how you got into this mess in the first place," Wilson said.

Both Gilbert and Jerry turned toward him almost in unison. "You don't understand," they parroted together.

Wilson turned away from them to look at Steve, and he could see the conflict and confusion on his face. He wanted to help them—that much was obvious to Wilson. "I think I do," Wilson said, answering their comment, but addressing it to Steve. "You don't owe them or anyone anything. They got themselves into this mess by blindly following your father. They never questioned what he wanted to do. They trusted wholeheartedly that he always had their best interests at heart and never double-checked. They went about their lives in happy oblivion, figuring someone else was taking care of them so they wouldn't have to, and now that their eyes are open, they want someone to come along and make it all better." Wilson glared at both men, daring them to contradict him. He knew he was right.

"How can you be so sure?" Steve asked him softly.

"Because I've seen it before," Wilson answered. "I had a... friend." Actually, a band member, but Gilbert and Jerry didn't seem to recognize him, and Wilson wanted to keep it that way. "Everything was always someone else's problem. If he made a mistake, there was always an excuse. Since I was the leader, it was usually me. After a while, the pressure began to build, and he began making more and more mistakes. He didn't show up when he should. He was making plenty of money, and we found out almost all of it was going up his nose." Wilson glanced over at the others to make sure they all understood. "The day we fired him for drug use, it wasn't his fault, but mine."

"We don't use drugs," Gilbert said indignantly.

"Maybe not. But you aren't taking charge of your own lives, either. Everything is still someone else's fault, and if you can just get the right leader, who'll make all the decisions, then you can go back to being completely oblivious once again. That way, when things go wrong, it isn't your fault, but someone else's," Wilson said, the words spilling out of him with more force than he intended. "Steve isn't your savior, and he doesn't owe you anything. His life is his own, and he can live where he wants and do what he pleases." Wilson's eyes bored into Steve's, hoping he was reading between the lines. Wilson knew he'd be devastated if Steve left, but it had to be Steve's decision. As much as Wilson wanted to ask him to stay… hell, he wanted to carry him into the bedroom, hold him tight, and never let him go, but he couldn't do that. Steve had to make up his own mind.

"It's okay," Steve said softly. "In the community, we always took care of one another, even when it was hard."

Wilson felt as though he could feel Steve moving away from him, being pulled back into the life he'd spent so much time and energy trying to get away from. He'd been starving when Wilson found him, and yet he seemed willing to go back with them. Wilson crossed his arms over his chest protectively, feeling like that was the only way to keep his heart from breaking. "You going to go with them?" he finally asked.

Steve turned, his expression blank until understanding seemed to dawn. "No. I have no interest in going back there. My father has been a control freak for a long time." Steve turned to Jerry and Gilbert. "If you think I can lead the community, then you're mistaken. I'm happy here, and I have a life and people who care about me and don't judge me."

"No one judged you," Gilbert said weakly, and Steve shook his head.

"You let my father judge me because you did nothing. Kyle and his family lost a home they loved because none of you would stand up for them." Steve shifted on the sofa, and Wilson felt his warmth where Steve touched his arm. "Whatever you want to do about my father is fine with me, but you and the other members of the community have to do it. I won't. It's time you stood up for what you want, or roll over and play dead again, the way you have for years." Steve stood up and walked toward the door. "I appreciate you coming by, if for no other reason than to let me know that Kyle is okay. He's a nice person who didn't deserve to be treated the way you did. Neither of us did. I know you didn't do those things yourself, but you condoned them." Steve looked strong as he stared down at the two larger men. "I wish you luck."

"Is that all?" Gilbert asked. "You won't change your mind?"

Steve shook his head definitively. "No. I have my own life now, and it isn't back there." Steve flashed Wilson a quick smile, and Wilson's stomach unknotted. "Drive back safely, and I hope you're able to do what you need to. I do want to ask that you not tell my father where I am. I don't want to see him, no matter what happens."

Gilbert stood up with a sigh, and Jerry followed right behind him. "We understand," Gilbert said, looking at Wilson and then back at Steve. "I'm still glad we found you. At least we know you're okay. And we have no intention of telling your father anything we don't have to." Gilbert stepped toward the door, and Jerry followed along. Steve shook hands with both of them as they walked outside. Wilson watched as Steve stood in the doorway. Through the open screen door, he heard the truck doors close and then the sound of the tires on the gravel drive as they pulled away.

"Do you really think they'll go?" Steve asked without looking toward Wilson.

"If they're telling the truth, which they seemed to be, then yes. There's nothing for them here," Wilson said as relief washed over him. Steve was staying here with him. "You're really going to stay?"

Steve closed the door and stepped to the sofa, plopping down next to him. "Yes. I like it here, and no matter what they might think, there's nothing for me back in the community but grief and pain. Living with my father, gay or not, was never a picnic, and now that I've been away from him, I feel like I'm free." Steve smiled broadly, and Wilson pulled him into a kiss that quickly deepened. They were just getting to the part where shirts were off and pants would be, as well, when someone knocked on the door. Wilson sighed and peered outside. A car was parked in the driveway. Groaning, he gave Steve a final kiss, and they redressed quickly.

"Just a minute," Wilson called, and then he buttoned his jeans. With one final look to make sure they were both presentable, he opened the door. Cheryl's smiling, heavily made-up face greeted him, and she held out what appeared to be a pie. Wilson thought he heard Steve growl behind him, but when he looked, all he saw was Steve walking toward the back of the house, and then he heard the sound of a door closing reverberating through the house.

"I thought we could get to know one another, so I baked you a cherry pie. You like cherry, don't you?" Cheryl said in a breathy voice, and it was all Wilson could do not to break out into laughter. Instead he took the pie.

"Thank you," he said haltingly, and he stepped back so she could come inside. Lord knew what he was going to do with her. She had the look in her eyes a fisherman gets when he thinks he's hooked the biggest fish ever, and Wilson shivered at the thought that in this case *he* was the fish. "I have some coffee on, would you like a cup?"

"I'd love one," she said, still using that imitation Marilyn Monroe voice that would sound comical if she weren't so completely determined. And Wilson knew he had to treat her nicely, because without a doubt, this was a woman who didn't like being scorned. She was hot and she expected every man to respond to her. If they didn't, there had to be a reason, and she'd find out what it was.

Wilson went into the kitchen, still carrying the pie, and set it on the counter before pouring two cups and carrying them back into the living room. Cheryl was half reclined on the sofa, her long legs and short skirt on display.

Cheryl was certainly using all the ammunition in her arsenal, but all it was doing was making Wilson uncomfortable. He knew he had to be careful in a friendly, but not too friendly sort of way. "So, what do you do, Cheryl?"

"I'm a waitress at the steakhouse in town," she answered with a huge smile, batting her brightly painted eyes slightly. "I'm one of the favorites there." Wilson could bet she was. Half the men in town probably requested her station, and the women steered their husbands away from her. "I just love your music," she added, leaning forward slightly, ostensibly to set down her coffee, but Wilson could see she was giving him a good look at her cleavage. He had to stop himself from rolling his eyes, and he quickly glanced around for some sort of distraction or excuse so he could get away, but there was nothing. "It's so warm and evocative," Cheryl added.

"I understand you have a son," Wilson said, trying to change the subject. After all, what mother didn't like to talk about her children?

"Yes. Carl's father didn't stick around for very long after he was born. Raising him alone has been difficult, and he needs a man in his life. Maybe he could come by and play with your maid's daughter, Alicia. She seemed like a wonderful little girl." Cheryl picked up her cup and slowly lifted it to her intensely red lips, all her motions exaggerated. Wilson had met many women like this in LA, but Cheryl seemed more intense and definitely more dangerous. This woman was feral, and the intense gaze she pinned on him had a "don't mess with me" message just below the surface.

Wilson heard the back door open and close, then Alicia walked into the room. Cheryl's expression went sour for a split second, and then her smile plastered back into place. Alicia opened the basket near the end of the sofa and pulled out a book. She showed it to Wilson, who smiled at her, and she walked to where he was sitting and handed it to him.

"Alicia, come in here," Maria called from the kitchen. "Don't bother Señor Wilson." Alicia looked disappointed, but left the room at a near run. She returned a few minutes later, sitting in one of the chairs, thumbing through the pages of the book, looking like she'd been scolded.

Wilson held out his hand to her, and she crawled onto his lap, still carrying the book. "I love a man who likes children," Cheryl said, and Wilson used that as an opening.

"I appreciate that. I usually read Alicia a story in the morning before we go for a ride. You're welcome to join us if you like," Wilson offered, and he saw the look in Cheryl's eyes shift.

She looked at her watch and stood up, brushing the imaginary wrinkles out of her skimpy red dress. "I should be going. Enjoy the pie, and stop into the steakhouse some evening. Maybe we can chat some more." She smiled brilliantly and slinked toward the door. Waving goodbye, she flashed him another smile that didn't quite go to her eyes before leaving.

Wilson had never been so relieved to see someone leave his home in his life. "You get ice cream this afternoon," he told Alicia before tickling her belly. She squirmed and laughed excitedly, and Maria came into the room.

"I asked you to leave Señor Wilson alone with his guest," Maria said, and Wilson peered up at her from his chair. Maria winked at him, and Alicia giggled once more like she was playing some game.

"Cheryl brought the pie on the counter," Wilson told Maria, who scoffed under her breath.

"Fake boobs, fake nose, and fake pie," Maria muttered. "She bought it at the grocery store." Maria sounded disgusted, and she turned and nearly stomped out of the room, still muttering about store-bought pies. Wilson had no illusions about where that pie was going to end up. He also knew that Cheryl might have left for now, but she was definitely going to be trouble. Taking the book from Alicia, Wilson opened the cover and began to read. Once he was done with the story, Wilson took Alicia out to the barn. Saddling up two horses and the pony, Wilson and Steve spent some time riding with Alicia in the ring. Being outdoors seemed to clear some of the lingering fog from Cheryl's visit, and by lunchtime, Wilson felt clearheaded and the music had begun to flow once again.

Chapter Eight

"ARE YOU still working?" Steve asked from the doorway, just as Wilson hit the send button on his e-mail. The music had played in his head, and the songs had been coming for the past two days. Something about Cheryl's visit had clarified for him exactly who he wanted, and it was the man standing in the doorway looking at him with adoration in his eyes.

"I'm almost done," Wilson answered with a smile. Both Howard and the record company were thrilled with his new songs. The real test would come when they played them before an audience. Then they'd see what the public thought of them. That was always the hardest part of the process. "I'll come to the barn, and we can—" Wilson's phone began to ring, and he snatched it up from where he'd set it on the desk. "Morning, Howard." Wilson held up a finger, asking Steve to wait a minute.

"What the hell is happening out there?" Howard asked in a bit of a panic.

"Excuse me," Wilson asked, a bit taken aback. "What are you talking about?"

"There are pictures of you on the front page of the supermarket rags. The headlines range from 'Meadows at Gay Party' to 'Meadows Assignation Among the Cars'. What the hell are you doing?"

"I went to a barbecue given by neighbors, nothing more. This is someone fishing," Wilson said, even as his stomach tightened. He hadn't done anything publicly at all, but someone had tipped off the media, probably for money, and it had to be someone who had been at Wally and Dakota's party. Not that he'd ever be able to find out who it was.

"You know they don't need anything to happen. The smallest item is blown out of proportion. Oh, and now you can expect every reporter between here and New York is on their way out there. I can arrange for some security if you like. At least we can prevent them from getting onto your property," Howard offered, and Wilson could feel the peace and quiet he'd been enjoying for the last few weeks slipping through his fingers.

"Go ahead, but make sure they know they are to be as unobtrusive as possible," Wilson said, and Steve looked at him curiously, clearly wondering what was going on. "Thanks."

"I'll see you this weekend, and we can assess things. In the meantime, don't give them any ammunition, whatever you do. Run your ranch and let them see you doing normal things. Let them see you riding and sitting on the porch with your guitar, things like that. Maybe we can defuse this before it gets too far." Howard was on a roll, and Wilson knew better than to interrupt, because it wouldn't do any good anyway. "I'm going to call the record company and have them put out some publicity about you spending quiet time working on your next album." Wilson figured he could hang up the phone and Howard would barely notice.

"Are you done?" Wilson asked in exasperation. "You saw the songs I've sent you. I wrote those because of the peace and quiet I have here. With the end of that comes the end of the music," Wilson warned, but Howard didn't seem to notice.

"We may as well make the most of this," Howard said. "Don't worry, I'll take care of everything and call you later. If we play this right, it can work to our advantage." Howard almost sounded gleeful as he hung up, and Wilson disconnected, dropping the phone to the desktop before resting his face in his hands. This was a nightmare. He'd bought the ranch to get away from reporters and the media hounds. He needed the quiet and a bit of peace so he could write. At least that was what he kept telling himself, but he knew better. As long as people stayed away and things were quiet, he could pursue Steve in relative safety with at least the outward image of having what he really wanted. Now, with everyone looking on and possibly trying to peer in his windows, he couldn't even touch him unless the lights were out. That wasn't fair to Steve.

"You all right?" Steve asked, moving into the room, strong hands settling on Wilson's shoulders, kneading his muscles.

Wilson rolled his neck, groaning at the welcome touch. "I don't know. Howard says that some hurtful things are being written about me. It seems someone sold some half truths about Wally and Dakota's party to the tabloids, and now they've printed a bunch of crap that has Howard all spun up." Wilson turned slowly in the chair. "He's arranging for security for the ranch, and he thinks we can expect a bunch of reporters to descend on us." Wilson knew he sounded as defeated as he felt. He wanted to reach out and hold Steve close, but he held back, knowing he needed to get used to being alone again. With all kinds of eyes around, he had to be even more careful.

Steve's hands fell away from him, resting at his sides. "Oh, I see." Without another word, Steve walked away, leaving Wilson alone in his office.

STEVE DROVE Wilson's truck around the vehicles parked near the driveway. A man walked in front of him, standing in the middle of the driveway, glaring at him. Steve sighed and pulled the truck to a stop right in front of him before slowly rolling down the window. "I don't care who you are," Steve began, "in two seconds I'm gunning the engine, and if you're still there, I'll run you down. You're trespassing and therefore committing a crime, so whatever happens to you is no concern of mine." Steve rolled the window back up, and after placing the truck in neutral, gunned the engine, and the man jumped out of the way. Steve put the vehicle in gear and sped up the drive to the house. For two days he'd been running the gauntlet whenever they needed something from town. Wilson had been largely holed up in the house except for when he went riding or came out to work in the barn.

A few times, Wilson had sat on the porch at dusk with his guitar. Steve knew he was supposed to be writing songs, but it wasn't happening, because all Wilson did was strum the strings. He didn't sing, and Wilson always did that when he was really working. In fact, not much had been happening around the ranch. Worse, over the past few days, Steve could feel Wilson pulling away more and more, withdrawing into himself, and Steve didn't know what to do about it. What hurt most was that at bedtime Wilson's door was closed now. The first night it had happened, Steve had gone as far as to lift his hand to knock, but stopped himself and went to his own room. Steve knew all this attention had Wilson unnerved, but he didn't have to push him away.

Steve got out of the truck and slammed the door, glaring down the drive toward where the trucks still waited. Reaching into the back, he grabbed a box of supplies and walked into the house. Maria was in the kitchen, and he set the box on the counter, and went back for another one. Wilson had gotten her a car to use, but she refused to drive through the "line of locos," as she called it. Steve retrieved the other boxes from the back of the truck without looking at the group out by the road. After dropping the rest of them in the kitchen, he went back outside to the barn. There was plenty of work to do, and he needed to remain busy or all he did was think… and pine over Wilson. He missed his touch and the way Wilson held him at night. He missed the other things too, but mostly he missed the way Wilson made him feel.

He pushed open the barn door and, after saddling Hunter, led him out to the ring. After setting up the jumps, Steve mounted and began taking the horse through his paces. He'd tried finding someone to help him train, but so far he hadn't had much luck. So he'd researched and conversed with people online, and he'd used their advice to begin. Hunter excelled at jumping, so much so that he could easily jump out of the ring. After training for a while, he spurred Hunter on and they did just that, the horse sailing over the fence, and then Hunter raced across the land, sailing with a smooth, flowing gait. This horse was spectacular, and Steve needed some time to think and feel free once again. The reporters made the ranch feel closed in, but on Hunter, Steve felt his heart and spirit soar. The horse seemed to love it, too, and Steve was reluctant to rein him in. But he had to eventually, so they turned around and walked back toward the barn, Hunter snorting his pleasure.

There was a strange car in the drive when he got back, and Steve knew that meant Howard must have arrived. Looking out toward the road, he saw the man talking to the reporters with lights and microphones thrusting toward him. He was welcome to them. Steve continued walking Hunter into the barn and unsaddled and brushed him carefully before turning the magnificent animal out into his paddock. After making sure the others were settled as well, Steve walked up to the house. As he made his way, he noticed that some of the reporters seemed to be packing up, and while others milled around, there was less activity and most of the people were talking on their phones.

Inside the house, he heard Wilson's and Howard's voices drifting down the hall. Then the sound was drowned as Maria started the vacuum cleaner. Steve wondered what was going on, but decided to give them their privacy instead. The whirring of the machine lasted awhile and then died away. Shortly afterward, Howard and Wilson's voices got louder as they approached, and they joined him in the living room. "Looks like some of them are leaving," Steve said, looking out the window as what appeared to be the last of the reporters drove away.

"I talked to them, and after two days of nothing to see but Willie riding horses and sitting on his front porch, they were growing bored," Howard said as he turned toward Steve. "So, you're still here."

Steve narrowed his eyes, looking at Wilson and then back at Howard. "I'm taking care of the horses."

"You realize you very nearly got Wilson outed."

Steve crossed his arms in front of his chest. "For your information, he *is* gay, and would coming out be such a bad thing? What's the worst that could happen? His father locking him in a basement room and then shipping him off to a facility to change him? Jesus, it's part of who he is, and all you want to do is pretend that part of him doesn't exist." Steve glowered at Wilson. "That's what you both want to do. You are who and what you are, Wilson. Sure, you have a right to privacy, but your behavior affects more than just you." Steve alternated his gaze from Wilson to Howard and then back again. Howard looked extremely uncomfortable, and Wilson appeared ashamed. "I'm sorry. I'll leave both of you to your business." Steve rose and walked down the hallway to his room. Behind the closed door, he sat on the edge of the bed. Maybe staying here wasn't such a good idea after all. Steve had broken away from under his father's control, and now he needed to be able to live open and happy. He'd already hidden his feelings before, and he wasn't about to do it again. Steve thought he loved Wilson, but he wanted someone who would love him back without reservations, like the way Wally and Dakota acted toward one another. Steve could hear voices traveling down the hall—voices that appeared to be arguing about something, and then they stopped.

Steve wasn't sure what he was going to do. Maybe Wally and Dakota would take him in for a while? That way Wilson could live his life without any threat or interference. Steve heard a soft knock on the door and got up to open it. Wilson stood in the hallway looking down and, quite frankly, tired. "What are you going to do?" Steve asked.

"I don't know," Wilson answered, and Steve walked around the bed. "I'm not sure what I can do." Steve heard Wilson walking toward him. "I understand how you feel, I really do, but I'm scared of how people will react. This coming out could end my career."

"Would that be so bad? You must have more money than you can ever spend, and people love your music. You can't get any peace unless you buy a ranch in the middle of nowhere." Steve turned toward Wilson. "I don't care if you're Willie Meadows or just Wilson—I want you to be happy and to see you really smile. You haven't done that in days, and I miss it. I miss you. Sure, I love it when you're singing and writing songs, because it makes you happy. If you came out, you'd be able to live your life for yourself… and maybe for me."

When Wilson didn't respond right away, Steve figured he had his answer. He'd been foolish to give his heart to Wilson. But he had, and he could feel it aching at the thought that Wilson didn't care about him the same way. "I understand. It's hard to face what you fear most, and it can have consequences you never expect." Steve knew that part firsthand, but he wouldn't change anything. Regardless of the hurt, pain, and fear, he knew being honest was the right thing to do.

Wilson sat on the edge of the bed, but Steve didn't look at him, staring at the wall instead.

"I'm scared," Wilson admitted softly. "What if who I am and everything I've done evaporates?"

Steve turned slowly. Wilson looked like he was about to curl into himself. He wrung his hands in his lap over and over. "I don't know what to do. I don't want to lose the career I've built, because I love the music, and performing is almost the greatest feeling ever." The bed bounced slightly as Wilson turned toward him. "I never needed drugs or anything like that because the rush and euphoria of having ten thousand people all calling for you, screaming your name, was the greatest high I could ever imagine." Excitement shone in Wilson's eyes, and momentarily Steve wished that excitement was for him. But he couldn't compete with ten thousand people or the adoration of crowds. He was just a kid trying to get away from his father who Wilson took in because he needed help.

"I guess I can see that," Steve mumbled, almost surprised at the depth to which Wilson's words hurt. He couldn't look at Wilson, and his gaze fell back to the wall.

"I used to think that performing was the greatest thing ever. That there was nothing better than hearing your name screamed by thousands," Wilson said, and Steve felt fingers touch his cheek. Blinking his watery eyes, Steve allowed his gaze to shift. "But that doesn't compare to one man calling out my name when we make love. Thousands of people cry out during each concert for a person who doesn't really exist, but it means more to me when you say my real name just once." Wilson cupped his cheek in his hand, and Steve leaned into the touch, needing it badly.

"What does Howard think?" Steve asked, knowing he was pushing it and he should probably just keep his mouth shut.

"He thinks I should go back to LA and everything will be fine the way it was, but I can't do that. I don't want to do that. My home isn't in LA anymore—it's here. But what Howard wants doesn't matter. He's my manager, and though it's his job to worry and fuss, in the end I make the decisions."

Steve nodded slowly. "So what are you going to do?"

"I don't know. But I'm not going to lie to anyone, and I haven't. I want to live my life honestly. I...." Wilson's voice trailed off, and Steve leaned closer.

"I know this isn't easy, and you don't have to make a decision today, but you need to figure out what you want, because you hurt me," Steve said. "Those reporters showed up, and suddenly I wasn't good enough or important enough anymore. You froze me out, afraid to look at me. You even shut me out of your bedroom, and I was beginning to think out of your heart too. All because of what someone printed without proof." Steve sighed loudly. "You let them win." Wilson's eyes widened in surprise, but Steve continued. "My dad may have thrown me in a basement room and then put me in a facility to change me, but I fought for who I was and I got away because I wasn't going to live a lie. You, on the other hand, have been living so many lies," Steve said, swallowing hard, "I'm not sure you're capable of living anything else."

"Give me some time," Wilson pleaded softly. "I need a chance to think this through."

Steve thought for a few seconds before leaning close, planting a light kiss on Wilson's lips. "I'll give you some time, but I won't wait forever. I want to live openly and honestly with the man I love, and I do love you, Wilson. But if that's not what you want, then you need to be honest with me." Steve could feel his insides rolling and turning. He'd told Wilson that he loved him and he desperately wanted to hear those words in return, but Steve knew he was just a kid, and Wilson was, well, Wilson.

"I've always been honest with you," Wilson said, "and I'm being honest with you now." Wilson moved closer, bringing their lips together once again. "I love you too, and I don't want to lose you. I understand how you feel, or at least I think I do, and I need some time to get my head around all this." Their kissing resumed and quickly deepened, with both of them falling back onto the bed, hands searching for warm skin.

An insistent knock interrupted them, and they both huffed softly before getting up. Wilson opened the door, and Steve saw him glare at his manager. "What is it?"

"Sorry, but Maria said that lunch was ready," Howard said sheepishly, and Steve felt his eyes as they shifted toward him. Steve felt Wilson take his hand and saw Howard's eyes widen, but he said nothing as they walked down the hall to the kitchen.

Most of the conversation at lunch centered on movie scripts and the shooting schedule, along with timeframe for getting Wilson's next album finished. Steve listened but stayed on the sidelines of the conversation. "The good thing about the movie is that it's being shot on location in South Dakota, with some studio work. Your part isn't huge, so you should be on location for about a month," Howard was explaining, and the realization hit Steve that Wilson was going to be gone for a whole month. Steve felt Wilson's hand slide into his under the table, and he squeezed it.

"That's fine, but what sort of accommodations will they provide?" Wilson asked.

"A location trailer as well as a hotel room in town. I already made sure both will have high-speed Internet so you'll be able to communicate." Howard kept looking at Steve suspiciously. "You will need to ride in this picture. There are horses, and you're playing a rodeo cowboy. The actual rodeo work will be done by a stunt man, but you'll need to be able to ride. That's the one stipulation in the contract."

Steve spoke up before Wilson could say anything. "He can. He's been working on it regularly, and we'll continue until he's ready to leave." There was no way Steve was going to let Wilson look bad, and he felt his hand being squeezed as Wilson gave him a wide smile. "He'll be able to do movie riding," Steve added, returning Wilson's smile before turning to Howard. "Maybe he could use his own horse. He's great tempered, and they're used to one another."

"I don't know about that. Maybe we should hire a riding coach," Howard said as he shoveled in some of Maria's fabulous tamales. He squeaked in surprise—and Steve smiled—when Maria whisked Howard's plate off the table.

"You show proper respect to Señor Wilson and Señor Steve or you no eat my food." Maria carried the plate to the counter, setting it down before glaring at Howard. It took every ounce of self-control for Steve to keep from laughing, and that lasted for two seconds before he broke down anyway.

"She's right," Wilson said. "Howard, relax. Everything will be fine. I enjoy riding and go two or three times a day. It helps with the songs." Wilson smiled, and Maria brought back the plate, giving Howard a scolding look that Medusa would have been proud of. "Now, you've told me the record company likes the songs I've written so far."

"Yes." Howard began eating again, but he kept glancing at Maria every once in a while. "They loved what you've written so far. The band is already working on tentative arrangements, and once you've got the rest and you're finished filming, you'll come to LA and begin rehearsals."

Wilson shook his head. "Absolutely not. Rehearsals will be done here. We can record in LA, but I'm not spending weeks away just to rehearse. The guys can stay in town, and I'm sure we can arrange for rehearsal space." Wilson set down his fork, the utensil clanking on the plate. "I have no intention of going back to LA unless I have to. The wide-open spaces are better for making music." Howard opened his mouth, and Steve saw Wilson glare at him. "Don't say anything, because that's just the way it is."

Howard glared back. "I was about to say that you may be right." Howard smirked slightly. "I can't deny that the songs you've written here are some of the best you've ever done. I'll arrange for the band to come here, and I'll see about places for them to stay. You need to find a rehearsal space. So when do you think you'll have the rest of the material ready?"

Wilson shrugged and sighed, shaking his head. "They'll be done when they're done."

"We could probably get the band out here in the next week or so to work on what's ready. You always have great ideas when you're making music," Howard offered, and Steve shifted his gaze to Wilson, seeing him nod. Steve wasn't so sure about having a bunch of people descend on them, but it was preferable to having Wilson leave.

They finished lunch, and Steve headed outside. For the time being, he'd had all he could stand of Howard and his sideways looks. Brushing Hunter until he shone, Steve saddled him and got ready to exercise him.

"Do you want some company?" Wilson asked from behind him, and Steve jumped slightly, Hunter stamping at his distress. Steve soothed the horse as he answered. "That would be great. I'll meet you in the yard."

Steve finished up and waited for Wilson. He looked down the drive and saw the black car from the security men Howard had hired. He hoped they would be gone soon. Wilson joined him, and after mounting, they rode back through the yard and across the rangeland behind the house.

"Are you excited about making a movie?" Steve asked as they walked slowly toward the trees that marked the creek.

"Actually, I am. It's sort of like making one of my childhood fantasies come true. As a kid, I always watched Westerns and wanted to be a cowboy. Now I get to play one in the movies." Wilson looked over at him, grinning from ear to ear. "I know I'll never be one for real. It has to be in your blood, and there's music in mine, but I get to pretend for a while."

Steve loved seeing Wilson smile. "I've been thinking. There's a lot of land that you aren't using. Maybe you could lease it to Dakota. Haven told me once that they're looking to expand, and we don't need all the land to raise horses. I bet they'd even let you work with them sometimes if you wanted. That way you could do real cowboy things."

Wilson moved his horse closer and pulled him to a stop. Steve did the same, their horses standing side by side. "The only cowboy thing I need to do is kiss one." Wilson leaned closer, his saddle creaking as his weight shifted. Steve moved to meet him, and they kissed, lightly at first, but then Steve felt Wilson's hand cup his head and the kiss deepened. Wilson's lips sucked lightly on his, and they continued until Hunter got impatient and began moving on his own.

"Do you have any idea how difficult it is to ride with a hard-on?" Steve asked, shifting slightly in the saddle, trying to find a comfortable position and failing. Wilson looked to be doing the exact same thing.

"I think we're both going to find out," Wilson quipped, and Steve shifted once again before guiding Hunter back toward the creek.

The air was cooler beneath the trees, and the slight breeze felt heavenly. Steve sat on Hunter, watching the water as it moved on its way to meet the river. "When your band gets here, what are you going to tell them?"

"So that's why you've been quiet most of the ride," Wilson commented. "I'm going to tell them the truth. I've known these guys for years, and if I can't trust them, then there's no one I can." Steve heard the fear in Wilson's voice. "I know it's the right thing to do. I just need to let the idea settle." Wilson shifted slightly in his saddle. "I just wish this was easier and that there wasn't so much at stake."

"I learned when I stood up to my father that the only thing that was really at stake was my own self-esteem. The things my father did to me were nothing compared to the things I did to myself when I hid who I was. Sure, you'll probably lose some friends and some of your fans, but you'll make new ones, and they'll like you for who you are, not who you pretend to be."

They continued walking their horses down the trail under the shade of the trees. "How'd you get to be so smart?" Wilson asked with a smile in his voice.

Steve pulled his horse to a stop. "Losing everything and everyone you thought loved you will smarten you up fast. I've learned a lot in the last few months. I found someone who knows who I am and loves me for it. I also found out who my real friends are, and you will too." Steve looked toward the house in the distance. "Howard is a complete pain in the ass, but he's there for you, no matter what. Part of the reason he's such a dick is because he really cares." Steve nudged his horse forward. "I suppose it's hard when you're famous to know who really cares and who's just hanging around because you are who you are."

"I know who my friends are and who cares," Wilson said firmly, and Steve turned, smiling at him. "You, for example, didn't even know who I was and you didn't care."

"And I don't now," Steve said. "To me, Willie Meadows is someone I don't know. He's a stranger. Wilson, on the other hand, is someone I've come to love and care for a great deal." Steve spoke from the heart, figuring it was time he laid his cards on the table. "I don't want anything from you, now or in the future, except...."

"I know what you want," Wilson said as he and his horse passed Steve, "and I want the same thing." Wilson spurred his horse forward, and they picked up some speed. Steve was confident that Wilson wouldn't go too fast or too far. Turning back toward the house, they sped up to a light canter, slowing as they approached the house.

Steve saw a car parked up near the house and a woman standing near the paddocks. He looked at Wilson and then back at her. "If that woman lays a hand on you, I'll poke her eyes out," Steve growled.

"I know what she wants, and she's not going to get it," Wilson said. "But I also don't want our business being broadcast all over the county. And Cheryl will do just that, I have no doubt."

Steve spurred his horse forward, racing into the yard, and Cheryl jumped back, nearly falling over. Steve kept the smile off his face as he dismounted and led Hunter inside. He didn't want to see her, and he didn't know what Wilson was going to do, but he'd made his feelings clear, which made him feel much better. She was Wilson's problem, and he was going to let him handle it, but he also intended to keep his eye on her.

After taking care of Hunter, he turned him out into his paddock and walked around to where he'd last seen Wilson. What he saw put a huge smile on his face: Cheryl stomping across the yard, yanking open the door to her car before speeding off in a cloud of dirt.

"I don't think we've seen the last of her," Wilson explained as he walked toward the barn.

"What did you say to her?" Steve asked as he watched her pull onto the road.

"That her time would be better spent with her son than trying to pursue me." Wilson looked seriously toward the road. "She wasn't happy, as you could see, and I have no delusions that we've heard the last from her."

Steve had little doubt that was true. He followed Wilson back into the barn and cleaned stalls while Wilson unsaddled his horse and sent him into his paddock. Once they were done taking care of the horses, Steve continued working until his chores were finished before heading to the house himself.

The rest of the day passed normally, and that evening, once he'd checked that the barn was buttoned up and the horses settled for the night, Steve headed to bed himself. Inside, the house was nearly quiet except for what sounded like soft music. It got a little louder the closer he got to his room. Wilson's door was open, and when he peered inside, Steve stopped, staring at the naked man lying on the bed. Wilson patted the bed in front of him. Steve was about to say something about meeting a closed door for the past few days, but the words slipped from his head when Wilson stood up, cock bobbing as he walked to where Steve stood. Taking him by the hand, Wilson drew him into the room, and the door closed silently behind them.

Steve only had eyes for Wilson, and in the dim room, he could see his lover's form tugging him forward, warmth spreading through his body as Steve's heart raced and his pulse thrummed through him. "Don't do that again," Steve murmured as his shirt slipped over his head and Wilson's chest pressed to his. "You cut me out because of fear."

"I know, and I'm sorry." Wilson slid his hands down Steve's back, sending a shudder through his body as he continued his trek lower, slipping fingers beneath his lover's belt. "I had a lot of time to think as I stared up at the ceiling, and I realized that I love you." Wilson kissed him, and Steve held his lover for support as his knees threatened to buckle under the searing onslaught. Steve stepped back under the intensity and hit the door. Wilson's body pressed to his, taking charge. Steve's head thunked back against the wood, and Wilson didn't let up. Steve's mind shut down and instinct took over. Wilson opened his belt, and the fabric of his jeans parted and then slid down his legs, pooling around his ankles. His underwear joined them, cool air flowing around his cock, but not for long.

Strong fingers wrapped around him, gripping and stroking. "Jesus God," Steve groaned, pressing himself back against the door so he didn't slide down it, his legs shook so badly with pent-up desire.

"Just stay where you are," Wilson whispered, and Steve nodded, rolling his head against the door, unable to form words. He could barely make a sound as he felt Wilson's lips on his neck, sucking and nipping, then on his chest, hot tongue swirling around his nipples, down his stomach, kissing a trail that had Steve's knees shaking.

"What are you gonna...?" The breath whooshed from his chest as Wilson engulfed him in a smooth sucking motion that brought Steve's hips away from the door. Wilson cupped his butt, squeezing his cheeks as he was sucked to within an inch of his life. "Fuck...," Steve whined, lifting his head to see what Wilson was doing, and he damned near cracked the door when Wilson bobbed his head and made small circles with a finger at his entrance. Steve tried to hold his hips still, but he ended up thrusting, and when he brought his hips back, Wilson slipped a finger inside him.

"You like that? You like it when I suck you and fuck you at the same time?" Wilson's deep, resonant voice dripped sex, and Steve tried to answer but ended up swallowing and gasping for breath. He made some pathetic sound, but Wilson seemed to understand, and as Steve moved his hips again, Wilson slid the finger deeper and wrapped his lips around his cock, sucking harder. Steve opened his eyes but saw nothing, so he closed them again. Wilson added a second finger, and Steve hissed softly as his muscles stretched to accommodate Wilson's long digits touching the spot inside him. Steve's knees gave out, and he slid down the door, landing on the floor in a heap. Wilson's fingers slipped from inside him, and Steve sprawled on his back on the floor.

All movement stopped. "I'm okay," Steve gasped, and Wilson gripped his cock just before Wilson sucked him deep once again. The floor gave him better purchase, and Steve thrust forward hard. Wilson let him move as Steve's body and instinct took over. Wilson stroked his skin, and every touch spurred him forward. The cold floor stood in stark contrast to the heat from Wilson's mouth. Steve's eyes clamped closed as he rode waves of sensation that threatened to overwhelm his brain. "Willie," Steve called, swallowing hard as he tried to breathe. "Don't stop." Steve could feel the tingling start at the base of his spine. He plastered his body to the floor, his fingers opening and closing, trying to find something to grip as the pressure continued to build. Wilson sucked hard, swirling his tongue around the shaft, and Steve saw stars. "Willie please, more, just a little more."

Wilson complied, sucking him hard and deep. Steve pressed his eyes closed as his entire body stiffened. Then he began to shake as his body went into overdrive. He knew he should be coming, but something in his brain made him hold off, and Wilson pushed him higher still, driving Steve to the pinnacle of body-wracking pleasure. When Steve couldn't take another second, he screamed and tumbled into the abyss, his mind numbing as his release shot through him.

Eyes closed, mouth open, breathing shallow, Steve slowly came back to himself. He didn't move, and Wilson seemed immobilized as well. Slowly, Steve felt the feeling return to his arms, and he carefully reached for Wilson, cradling his head in his hands. "I love you," Steve murmured into the darkness.

Wilson shifted and kissed him, and Steve tasted his own salty flavor on Wilson's tongue. "You called me Willie."

It took Steve's addled mind a few seconds to understand what Wilson was saying. "I didn't mean *him*," Steve said, referring to Wilson's Willie Meadows persona. "You're my Willie, and my Wilson, and if I call for Willie, it's you, always you."

Wilson kissed him again and then stood up, tugging Steve to his feet. They didn't have far to go and then they were falling again, this time onto a soft mattress. Wilson vibrated with excitement as Steve felt his lover's weight press him against the mattress. Then he stopped, and Steve heard a drawer open and close. "I want you, love," Wilson groaned with renewed excitement. "Roll over, it'll be easier for you."

Steve complied and felt hot kisses trail down his back and over his butt cheeks. Hot hands parted his cheeks, and Steve arched his back, making soft, mewling sounds as Wilson's tongue slid over him, probing his entrance. Steve had barely recovered from a mind-blowing orgasm not five minutes earlier, and already Wilson was making his body sing again. A slicked finger slipped into him, and Steve groaned, loving the way Wilson felt and the way he touched deep inside him.

The room filled with all kinds of sounds, and it took Steve a few seconds before he realized they were all coming from him. Wilson rimmed him until his head throbbed, and then long fingers filled him. Steve squirmed on the bed, his dick already hard again, sending shocks of desire through him every time he moved. "Are you ready for me?" Wilson whispered into his ear before sucking it, his body covering Steve's.

"God, yes. Fuck me," Steve cried, begged, pleaded, damned if he knew—the words were out of his mouth before he could think about them. Steve felt Wilson's weight shift and heard a package open. His hands slipped beneath the pillow, touching the headboard, hips rocking slightly in sweet anticipation. The bed rocked slightly, and Wilson's warmth slipped away. Steve whined softly, and then he felt Wilson pressing against his entrance. At first he wasn't sure he could take him, but then his body opened and Wilson pressed inside. Steve hissed through his teeth as his muscles stretched. He almost asked him to stop, but the burn soon transformed into bliss, and Wilson sank deeper into him.

He could feel every ridge, every throb of Wilson's cock as he slid into his body. Steve felt so full, and as Wilson buried his thick length inside him, the sensation threatened to overwhelm him.

"Breathe, sweetheart," Wilson crooned into his ear as he stilled. Steve felt Wilson's weight press on him, his warmth covering him. Steve's butt throbbed and pulsed as he got used to the invasion. Then, slowly, Wilson began to move, withdrawing, his cock dragging over a spot that sent a zing down Steve's spine. Equally slowly, Wilson pressed back inside, and Steve groaned from deep in his throat, drawing it out until Wilson stilled once again.

"I want to see you," Steve moaned softly between panting breaths, and Wilson withdrew before helping Steve roll onto his back. Wilson lifted Steve's legs, positioning them so his ankles rested on Wilson's shoulders, and entered him again. This time it was with a single, long movement. Steve's eyes had become used to the darkness, so now he could see Wilson's face, and he concentrated on Wilson as they moved together. Wilson stroked his chest and sides as he moved deep within him. Steve's desire had waned for a few minutes, but it came roaring back, and he stroked himself as the pace of their lovemaking built.

"You feel amazing around me," Wilson told him as he leaned forward, meeting his lips in a sloppy kiss. "You're like a furnace, tight and amazingly hot."

Steve smiled and kissed him again as Wilson drove deep inside him. Holding his lover tight, Steve gave himself completely into Wilson's care, trusting his lover, and what an amazing feeling it was. He knew Wilson would take care of him, and as soon as he let go, he felt Wilson driving his climax higher and higher. Wilson's rhythm became erratic and uncoordinated. Steve felt his own climax build as his body began to tingle. Forcing himself to keep his eyes open, Steve screamed Wilson's name as he came onto his stomach, feeling Wilson's cock jumping and throbbing deep inside him.

Steve gasped for air, flopping back on the bed once his orgasm had passed, the warm afterglow still tingling through his body as their bodies separated. Wilson slipped off the bed and then quickly returned and hugged him tight as the effects of their lovemaking lingered between them. Steve felt as limp and pliable as a noodle, and as happy as he could ever remember. Wilson had told him he loved him, and as he remembered, he squeezed his lover tight.

"Um, Steve, I can't breathe," Wilson told him with a smile in his voice, and Steve loosened his grip, yet still held Wilson firmly, enjoying the hairy roughness as their legs entwined, the warmth of Wilson's chest, and the smoothness of his lover's butt cheeks as he stroked them with his fingers. Steve closed his eyes, utterly contented and happy.

A ringing sounded in the room, and Steve blinked his eyes open. Wilson jerked and then stilled as Steve answered. "Hello."

"Steve, it's Wally. We just got a very strange phone call from someone who knows you. They couldn't find your number, so they called us, for some reason. They said they saw you at our party and that they know you from the community."

"Did they leave a name?" Steve asked, moving to get out of the bed so he wouldn't disturb Wilson, but a hand on his shoulder stopped him, and he felt the bed shift and then strong arms wrapped around his chest, with a stubbly cheek resting on his shoulder.

"He said it was Gilbert and he left a number." Wally told it to him. "He said it was urgent and asked for your number, so I gave it to him. I hope that's okay."

"Thank you," Steve said, now wide awake. "It's fine." Wally said good night and disconnected. The phone rang again almost immediately, and Steve answered it, only to wish he hadn't.

Chapter Nine

SINCE STEVE'S late-night phone call, they'd been on pins and needles for almost a week. Add to that the fact that his band was set to arrive at almost any time, and Wilson couldn't sit still, no matter what. He'd tried writing, but what little he'd come up with sounded completely depressing. He and Steve had continued to ride, but they stayed close to the house, and though Wilson had hoped to let the security Howard had hired go, after that call, he'd asked them to stay on for a while. He had to give them credit— John and Marty were good at their jobs. They were around, but never got in the way, and there were times he would forget about them. That is, until he'd see one of them emerge from around the corner of the house or come out of the barn.

"When will they arrive?" Steve asked, coming out of the house to stand next to him on the porch.

"Anytime," he answered as his phone began to ring. He saw Howard's number and answered it. "They aren't here yet."

"I'm not calling about the band, but to tell you the shit is about to hit the fan. It seems that someone has sold a picture of you and Steve to one of the entertainment magazines in town, and they're going to run the story. The only reason I know about it is because I was called for a quote, which I refused to give. I haven't seen the picture, but it's being billed as you two on horseback together kissing." Howard sounded furious. "I told you to be more careful!"

Wilson's stomach turned over, and for a second he thought he was going to be ill. Then Steve's hand settled on his shoulder, and the clouds that had covered his mood cleared and he could think straight. "When do you think they'll publish?"

"In the next three days, why?" If he didn't know better, Wilson would have thought Howard had been drinking.

"I need to think things through. I'll call you tomorrow and let you know what I want to do." Wilson waited for Howard's retort, and he didn't have to wait very long.

"There's nothing to decide. We need to deny it and then keep our mouths shut. Maybe we could find a woman you could be seen with in LA for a few weeks." Howard seemed to be on a roll, and Wilson couldn't get a word in edgewise.

"Howard!" Wilson finally snapped. "As I said, *I'll* decide what I want to do. Give me until tomorrow, and I'll let you know what I want done. Until then, keep quiet and say nothing." Wilson softened his tone. "I know how you feel, Howard, but this is my life, and I need to decide how I'm going to live it."

Howard remained quiet for a few seconds. "I know. You take your time. You know I'm behind you, no matter what. I'll call you tomorrow. Let me know if you need anything." Howard disconnected, and Wilson put the phone back in his pocket. He sighed and looked over toward the barns and the horses in their paddocks.

"What's wrong?" Steve asked quietly after a while, and Wilson debated telling him anything. He didn't want to upset him, and this was something he needed to decide on his own. But he knew that wasn't fair to either of them.

"Someone is about to publish a picture of us on horseback, kissing, and they contacted Howard for a quote, which he refused to give," Wilson explained tiredly.

"What are you going to do?" Steve asked, and Wilson was about to answer when a car, followed by another, pulled into the drive.

"I'm not totally sure yet, but the ideas are forming." Wilson turned to Steve. "I'm not going to hide, I can tell you that. But I need a little time to think this through." The cars pulled to a stop and doors opened.

"You made it, Hammer," Wilson called when he saw the drummer. He'd know him anywhere. The man was bald, and the member of the group he'd always been closest to. Peter, the bassist came next, pulling Wilson into a hug, and then followed his guitarist, Freed. These were the main members. When they were on tour, there were dozens of others who took care of everything from setup to takedown to sound mixing. But at this point, all he needed were these three men. Before going inside, Wilson turned, "Guys, this is Steve. He takes care of most things around here."

They each shook hands, and Wilson led everyone inside. "Maria has lunch on, and this bundle of energy is Maria's daughter, Alicia." Wilson bounced her, and she giggled before running off to her toys when he placed her back on her feet.

The table was set and everyone sat down. Wilson noticed Steve standing away from the others, looking at him questioningly, and Wilson motioned him to the table.

"Willie, there's something we need to ask you," Hammer began as soon as he sat down. "There are a lot of rumors...." Hammer looked at the others, who nodded.

"I know," Wilson began. He looked at Steve, who nodded his encouragement, and the others stilled, their eyes flowing to Steve.

"So it is true?" Peter commented. "You're gay." Wilson nodded. He'd already determined that he wasn't going to lie, so he waited to see what the reaction of the men would be. He hoped they would accept him and be happy that he was happy, but he wasn't sure. He'd known all of them for years, and he hoped they would be okay with him now. "Is Steve your lover?"

"He's my boyfriend, yes," Wilson answered honestly, looking from person to person for some sort of indication about how they felt. But he couldn't see anything in their eyes, and that disturbed him. Maybe this wasn't going to go as well as he'd hoped it would.

"So this is who you really are?" Hammer asked, and Wilson nodded slowly.

"I'll understand if you can't accept it."

"Accept it," Hammer echoed. "I've been wondering when you were going to face up to it yourself." Hammer stared at him hard. "We've all known for years but said nothing because you never said anything."

Wilson looked around the table, and the other two men nodded.

"We want you to be happy, man," Freed said, his chiseled face breaking into a smile. "And we've all seen the music that's come out of you these last few months. It's amazing, and we figured you had to be happy to be writing stuff like that."

Wilson released the breath he'd been holding and smiled, locking eyes with Steve, who smiled as well.

"But," Freed continued, "while it doesn't matter to us, we can't speak for the fans. I suspect that a certain part of the fan base will evaporate." The others shrugged, and Wilson chewed his lower lip. "There's nothing to be done about it, though. I think we're all better off being truthful."

Maria brought plates and sandwiches to the table. "If you want my opinion," Maria said quietly, and Wilson smiled and nodded. "You may get new fans you haven't had before."

"That's true," Peter agreed. "If you ask me, whatever you do, make sure it's done in a way that makes it clear that you aren't ashamed of who you are." Peter took a bite of his sandwich and then set the rest on his plate. "What does Howard think of all this?"

"You know Howard—he wants everything to stay as it is," Wilson said, and the others nodded.

"Well, it can't," Steve commented, and everyone looked at him, including Wilson. "Just having this conversation means that things have changed. Secrets have a way of getting out."

"He's right," Hammer said. "It's better to control the message than to let someone else do it." Heads nodded around the table.

"But you have to do what you think is right. We can give you advice, but it's your life and your decision."

"It affects all of us, though," Wilson explained, knowing that whatever decision he made would have an effect on everyone seated around the table. If it were just him, the decision would be easier, but it wasn't. The livelihood of every person around the table depended upon him.

"Yes, it does," Freed said, "but that doesn't mean you shouldn't do what's right. We've been making music a long time, and I for one don't want to do anything else with anyone else. We've all done well enough that we'll survive whatever you decide." Heads nodded once again, and then everyone lapsed into silence.

Wilson tried to breathe evenly and calmly, but his heart was going a mile a minute. He could hardly believe what the guys had told him. Looking at Steve, he saw his lover's smile and then he felt Steve squeeze his leg reassuringly. Whenever he'd imagined this conversation, he's always pictured yelling and disappointment, and he'd really expected the guys to bail on him. So their acceptance meant more than he could ever say. He knew his surprise was written on his face, but thankfully the guys ignored it and continued eating.

"So what kind of place do you have for us to rehearse?" Freed asked as he finished yet another sandwich. The man was tall, thin, and ate like a horse.

"The VFW has agreed to let us use their hall. The acoustics aren't bad, and there's plenty of space for us to set up and work." Wilson finished his sandwich before getting up to take his dishes to the kitchen. The others followed suit and then headed outside to the vehicles. "I'll be with you in a minute."

The guys left, and Wilson stood with Steve. "I'm glad it seems to be working out," Steve said, but there was little joy in his voice, the worry lines around his eyes getting deeper.

"Me too," Wilson agreed. "Do you want to come with us?" He hated the thought of leaving Steve behind. For the past week, he'd kept a close eye on his lover, and they'd both been on edge ever since Steve had received that phone call.

"No. I have things I need to do here. Maria and Alicia will be here, and the security men are always around. I'll be fine," Steve told him. Wilson didn't think he looked fine, and was about to argue, but knew it wouldn't do any good.

"I'll call you, I promise," Wilson said. Steve pulled him into a hug and then kissed him before leaving the house. Wilson followed, and Steve waved as he walked to the barn. Wilson watched as he walked, tight cowboy butt swaying as he moved. Once Steve disappeared inside, Wilson climbed into his truck and led the guys into town.

He was careful not to lose them as he led their small caravan to the hall. They piled out and began unloading their instruments. "I can't remember the last time I hauled my own stuff," Hammer commented as he pulled a large drum from the backseat.

"Out here we do a lot for ourselves," Wilson commented as he pulled his guitar and amp from behind his seat. "I've even cleaned stalls." When Wilson closed his door, he found three sets of eyes looking at him skeptically. "Okay, once, I did it once," Wilson confessed with a smile. "But I have learned to ride, and this fall I'll help the neighbors move cattle." Wilson picked up his instrument and unlocked the door, leading them inside. "As I said, it's not bad."

"You've really gone local, haven't you?" Peter asked as he carried in a load of equipment, setting it down before starting to set up. They'd brought largely acoustic instruments for their work session.

"I guess," Wilson answered as he helped get things ready.

"To be honest, I'm probably a little jealous," Peter told him before returning his attention to what he was doing.

In a relatively short period of time, they were set up, ready, and began warming up. They began with some of their standards, songs as familiar as old friends. Once they were comfortable, they moved into some of the new material. They'd worked through one song and started on "Long, Lonely Nights" when Wilson called a halt. "It isn't working," he explained. "It doesn't sound right."

"It's what you wrote," Hammer countered.

"I know," Wilson agreed. "But I may have left something out." Wilson began pacing the floor still carrying his guitar. "It sounds flat, and I don't know why." Wilson closed his eyes and blocked out everything, thinking back to the night he'd written this song sitting on the porch. Darkness fell around him, and he could hear the song playing in his mind. "It needs nature's accompaniment," he said out loud and then turned back to the guys.

"What the hell does that mean?" Hammer asked with a grin.

"When I wrote it, I was sitting on the porch. There were crickets and the sound of horses stomping, the breeze blowing around the house. That's what the song needs." Wilson grinned.

"How do we do that?" Peter asked skeptically. "Do you want to record them and add the sounds to the track?"

"No. I'm thinking we bring in a fiddler on this number, let him approximate the sound, and Hammer, you can add the stomp of a horse with the drums." Wilson set down his guitar and walked back to him. Taking Hammer's place, he began to play with the large drum. "It's the way the horse stomps and then scrapes his hoof along the ground. It doesn't have to be exact, because most people won't understand, but it's part of the feel. This song should feel like you're sitting on the porch thinking of the one you love."

Wilson could hear the music playing in his head just the way he wanted it, and after explaining as best he could, they began to play. The instruments overlaid the music in his head, and everything fit together. There were pieces missing, but it was working, and then he began to sing the words he'd written while imagining not having Steve in his life any longer. He sang of dark hair and bright eyes, and how it felt when they settled on him. Everything fell into place as they played, and once the song ended, the room fell silent as the last note faded away. No one moved, and Wilson wondered what was wrong. Then he heard three voices each mutter, "Fuck...." Wilson felt a tingle go up his spine, and he frantically made notes on his music.

"That was amazing," Freed commented as Wilson finished his notes. The others were doing the same. "Let's try it again," he added happily, and they began to play. They finished the song, and Wilson felt that same tingling he had before. Adding a few notes, he was about to suggest they move on when his phone vibrated in his pocket. Pulling it out, he saw the house number and answered it.

"Is everything okay?" Wilson asked immediately, and he heard Maria chuckle.

"Everything is fine. Señor Steve asked me to call. He said he was going to exercise Hunter and that he would call you when he gets back."

"Thank you," he said and hung up, shoving the phone back into his pocket. He wished Steve had called himself because he'd have liked to hear his voice. "Ready for 'Walking Away from Me'?" Wilson asked as he walked to where the guys waited. "I envisioned this one being intimate and soft, sort of a lament for something precious that's just out of reach."

The guys looked at each other. "That's not what Howard said when he sent it to us. He said the record company wants to play this one big. They think it's the hit of the album," Freed told him. "I think it's the one we just did, but you know them, they have to stick their nose in."

Wilson knew, and in the past they'd been right, but Wilson didn't think they were this time. "Let's try it both ways. We do it their way first and see which one works for us. Then I'll sic Howard on the record company, if necessary." They agreed, and did the song the way the record company wanted. It sounded good and it worked, but Wilson didn't really feel it. Then Wilson pulled up a stool from the bar in the corner and began to strum his guitar. The others joined in, slowing the tempo, and Wilson sang through the song, ending with, "Your long legs walking away from me, walking away, walking away, walking away from me." Tingles shot up and down his spine. Wilson could barely sit still as he played the final chords and let the music fade away.

"You wrote that for Steve, didn't you?" Freed asked from behind him, and Wilson nodded once.

"I wrote them all for him," Wilson explained before turning around. Freed wiped his eyes, and Hammer looked down at his drums, refusing to look at anyone. Peter fiddled with the strings on his bass. "Okay, what did you think?" Wilson asked, but no one answered him.

"Sic Howard on them," Freed finally said, and the others nodded their agreement. Wilson knew that was what he wanted to do, as well, but it felt right that they thought the same thing. Wilson made notes on both renditions of the song.

"I think we've had enough for today," he suggested, and the others readily agreed. Normally they would work for hours, but Wilson could see they were tired. "We can leave anything here we need. I've been assured that no one will be in here until this weekend." Wilson's phone vibrated again, and he pulled it out.

"Señor Wilson." Maria sounded panicked. "Señor Steve's horse came back without him. I asked the security men to see if they could find him. They're looking for him, but I'm worried something has happened." She sounded close to tears.

"We're on our way back now." Wilson hung up and shoved the phone into his pocket, already heading toward the door. "Steve's missing, and I need to get back now." He was at the door, searching for his keys, by the time he'd finished talking. The guys followed him outside.

"The door's locked," Hammer said as they hurried to the cars. "We'll be right behind you." Wilson climbed inside, started the engine, and took off, calling the police as he drove. He didn't have much to give them other than what Maria had said, but they said they'd send someone right out.

Wilson drove like a bat out of hell, flying down the rural roads. A truck came at him as he turned a corner, driving equally fast. Wilson caught a glimpse of a head leaning against the passenger window through the truck windshield and stomped on the brakes. He was damned lucky the truck didn't flip as he whipped it around and took off. He'd know that head anywhere, and he was positive Steve was in that truck. He passed the guys and kept going, picking up his phone and calling the police again. "I'm heading toward town on Old Cheyenne Road," Wilson told the dispatcher. He tried to explain to the dispatcher what he thought was happening but gave up, throwing the phone on the seat, and continued driving. Approaching town, the truck in front of his slowed as traffic thickened. The driver swerved around another car and took off.

His phone rang, and Wilson pressed the speaker button as he tried to get around the slower car. "Mr. Edwards, this is Officer Carlston, where are you?" The deputy sounded pissed, but Wilson didn't really care. If that was Steve, he was hurt and in trouble. That was all that concerned him.

"I'm approaching town on Old Cheyenne. I can just see the blue truck turning at the main intersection. He appears to be headed toward the freeway. I believe my boyfriend has been kidnapped and is in that truck." The words were out of his mouth before he could think about them, and he continued driving.

"We'll get him, don't worry. I'm coming up on him." The line disconnected, and Wilson slowed down, but continued driving in the direction he'd seen the truck heading. He continued through town and out toward the freeway. As he got close, he saw flashing lights and began to breathe easier. Pulling up behind one of the cars, Wilson got out and approached one of the officers.

"Did you stop him?" Wilson asked without preamble.

"Yes, but I don't think they're who we thought they were. It's a man taking his son to the hospital," the deputy explained. "We've called an ambulance, and they're on their way."

Wilson had felt so sure it was Steve in that truck. He was about to turn around, but he knew he needed to see for himself. Walking past the cruiser, he approached the truck and saw Steve lying on the seat. He rushed to him.

"You get away from my son!"

Wilson turned and met the eyes of Steve's father. The man stared back, and Wilson instantly knew he was looking at a man used to being obeyed and used to wielding power over others. It was unsettling and more than a little intimidating, but Wilson knew how to handle men like him and didn't back down.

"Sir," one of the deputies said firmly. "You need to step away."

"That is my boyfriend, Steve," Wilson said, looking into the car. "And this man is a kidnapper. He might be his father, but Steve does not want to go anywhere with him."

The sheriff's deputies looked at one another, confused.

"When Steve told his father he was gay, that asshole threw him into a basement room and then shipped him off to some crackpot hospital so they could change him. He does not want to go with him, and I bet you'll find that whatever is wrong with Steve, he did to him." Wilson could feel his agitation rise, and he pressed by the officer, approaching Steve, gently wiping the hair from his forehead. "You're going to be okay. I promised I wouldn't let him take you, and I won't."

"Sir," the deputy next to him said. "I can't do much without hearing from the injured man."

"You most certainly can't let Steve go anywhere with him," Wilson said as he carefully held Steve's hand, being very careful not to move Steve in case he was hurt. Steve looked so pale, and when Steve's father approached, Wilson moved to stand between him and Steve. "Don't come any closer. I know what you did, and I won't let you hurt him anymore."

"He's my son, and I know what's best for him," Steve's father growled.

"Does that include locking him in a basement room and throwing him into a hospital because he was gay?" Wilson tried to keep his voice level, but it wasn't working.

"He's sick and he needs help. They could cure him."

"So you admit it," Wilson pressed, looking at the police officers. "The last I heard, the AMA does not classify homosexuality as a disease, and since I doubt you're a doctor, you don't get to make those decisions." Wilson turned to the deputies. "This man just confessed to kidnapping. His son is an adult, and he does not get to make decisions for him."

The deputy approached Steve's father. "Put your hands where I can see them."

"I'm not going anywhere," Steve's father protested, and two deputies grabbed his hands, forcing him to the ground.

"It looks like you are now," Wilson commented before returning his attention to Steve, who seemed to be stirring. "Steve, it's me," Wilson said, taking his hand, watching as Steve's head lifted off the seat. "Take it easy, help is on the way." Sirens sounded, quickly getting louder. "You're going to be fine."

"My father took me," Steve said hoarsely, and Wilson watched as Steve moved to the edge of the seat, vomiting violently onto the floor. Wilson held his hand until the EMTs arrived and took charge of the situation. Wilson watched as Steve was helped out of the truck and then loaded into the ambulance. Wilson stepped back as the doors closed, and after a few minutes the ambulance pulled away. Wilson watched it go before turning his attention to the deputies.

"What do you need to know?" he asked, and then the questions began. Wilson told them everything he knew about the relationship between Steve and his father, his anxiety increasing with each passing second until they let him go and he was able to drive back toward town and the hospital.

"DO YOU need help?" Wilson asked Steve before opening his door and hurrying around to Steve's side, pulling open his door and taking his hand.

"I'm not helpless," Steve told him, though Wilson ignored his mild protest and helped him toward the front door. Inside, both Maria and Alicia fussed over Steve, with Alicia sitting next to Steve as soon as he sat down on the sofa. "I'm okay," Steve told Alicia, but she didn't seem convinced, crawling onto his lap, and Steve hugged the little girl to him. "I really am," he told the assembled room.

"What happened?" Freed asked, and Steve told the band members what his father had done to him.

"About a week ago, I got a call from Gilbert, one of the men from the community where I grew up, and he told me that they'd removed my father as leader. Gilbert also said that my father blamed me for his ouster and that my father had left and they didn't know where he'd gone. They were afraid he would come after me." Steve coughed, and Wilson jumped up to get him a glass of water. He handed Steve the glass and settled next to him on the sofa. Steve sipped the water and then placed the glass on the table. "Gilbert told me that they hadn't told my father where to find me, but they were still concerned."

"What happened today?" Wilson asked nervously.

"I was riding Hunter back toward the ranch when I was pulled off him. I remember falling and then hitting the ground. Then I sort of came to and someone gave me something to drink. It tasted fruity, and I didn't think much about it. My mind wasn't working too well. After that I don't remember much until I heard your voice arguing with my father and the police officers."

Maria lifted Alicia off Steve's lap and carried her out of the room.

Steve turned to him, and Wilson saw an expression he couldn't read. "I heard what you said. I couldn't move, but I heard you. You told them I was your boyfriend."

"You are," Wilson said.

"I know. But you told them and everyone else." Steve rested his head against Wilson's chest. "Whether you know it or not, you came out for me."

"I love you," Wilson whispered. He distantly heard the others stand up and leave the house quietly, to give them their privacy, and he barely heard the car engines start as the guys drove away. "I was so concerned about you. I didn't stop to think what I was saying. All I knew was that I couldn't let your father take you anywhere." Wilson's heartbeat sped up as he thought of what could have happened to Steve if he hadn't seen him and gone after him the way he had. What if he'd been just a few minutes later? Or if they'd gone a slightly different route home? The thoughts scared him.

"Do you regret what you said?" Steve lifted his head, his eyes filled with concern.

"No. I'd already decided that I wasn't going to hide anymore. You're my boyfriend, lover… whatever the proper term is, and I won't deny you again." Wilson stroked Steve's soft hair, his hand gently cradling Steve's head. "I almost lost you today, and I realized that you are more important than my career or legions of fans. No matter what, I can still make music, and that's what I really love. If you're the only one around to hear it, then I have all the audience I really want." Wilson leaned closer, touching his lips to Steve's. Once he pulled away, Steve blinked up at him before smiling.

"Do you know what's going to happen to my father?" Steve asked softly, and Wilson shook his head.

"He was taken into custody, but that's all I know. I did ask that they pursue possible kidnapping charges, and they seemed to think they could make those stick, but as for the other things he did, there's very little proof other than your word." Wilson saw the pain well in Steve's eyes. "Either way, he's not going to be around for quite a while." Wilson managed a smile, and Steve seemed to accept his assurances. Wilson had every intention of making sure Steve's father wouldn't be able to terrorize his son again. "You should probably lie down for a while." Wilson stood up and extended his hand, helping Steve to his feet. "The last of whatever your father put in that drink he gave you needs to get out of your system." Wilson helped Steve down the hall to his bedroom, guiding him down onto the large bed. "Are you hungry?"

Steve shook his head, and Wilson helped undress him before settling him under the covers. Wilson leaned over Steve, kissing his cheek before quietly leaving the room. Steve was already half asleep by the time he left the room, and once Wilson was down the hall, he fished out his phone and placed a call to Howard.

"I have some things I need you to take care of," he said as soon as Howard answered. "I'm turning you loose on the record company to get me the arrangement I want for 'Walking Away From Me.' We all agree that acoustic is better, so give them hell."

"They were adamant the last time I talked to them, but I'll try."

"Good. And I want you to get me on a sympathetic daytime talk show before that article is set to run. I want to tell my story." Wilson tamped down the butterflies that threatened in his stomach. "I want to control the message. It's time I stopped hiding. The band and I have already talked it over, and they agreed."

Wilson heard Howard sigh. "If you're sure about this," Howard began.

"I'm sure. The chips can fall where they may, but I'm sure that I want to live my life in an honest way with the man I love. He deserves that, and so do I." Wilson smiled to himself. "I know you have your concerns, and so do I, but think of it like this—all our lives will be easier."

At first Howard didn't say anything, then he said, "I'm with you the whole way. I'll also let the record company know what's going on. They have a right to know, and I have to warn you, they might want to renegotiate your contract, and the movie role may evaporate, as well."

"I know, and if they do, then that's fine. But I don't think being gay is as big a deal as it once was. There are openly gay actors on television, and there have been openly gay musicians for years. Tell whoever you need to, but also tell them that I will not renegotiate contracts. If they want out, then we'll let them out and we'll shop another record company. They'll back off."

Howard's chuckle drifted through the phone. "If I'd been the one with your talent, you'd have made one hell of a manager. Let me make those calls, and I'll let you know what I find out."

"Thank you," Wilson said before hanging up.

He wandered around the house, worrying about Steve and the other decisions he'd made. For the first time he could remember, he was second-guessing himself.

"Señor Wilson, it will be fine," Maria said when he wandered into the kitchen. "You are a good man and you are doing the right thing. Lies are never good. They only hurt and make you unhappy."

Wilson nodded his agreement and kissed her lightly on the cheek before walking back down the hall to his bedroom. Steve was sound asleep, and after watching him for a long time, Wilson closed the door behind him, his mind quieter and at ease. He had done the right thing; he knew that in his heart. Going outside, he retrieved his guitar from his truck and sat on the porch. Sitting in one of the chairs Steve had redone, Wilson strummed his instrument and let his feelings loose. Tears of joy and relief welled in his eyes, and happiness bloomed in his chest.

Then music began to play in his head, and Wilson let it free. Up till now, it had been soft and comforting, but what came now was raucous and loud, feeding off the turmoil of emotion he'd been through in the last few hours. Energy from the music came in waves and flowed out through his fingers and hands. Then it calmed, filling him in a way that was hard to describe, settling in his heart and staying there, shifting into a love song.

Wilson had written many songs in his life, and a few had even approximated love songs, but this one stole his breath away. He sang it to Steve, even though he was still asleep, and then he sang it again, the words changing slightly until he had them just right. Then he sang it one last time, his voice floating through the early evening air. He sang it to the horses and any other living thing within shouting distance. He loved Steve, and he wanted the world to know.

"Is that for me?"

Wilson stilled, the sounds fading away as he turned and saw Steve standing just behind him. Wilson nodded slowly. "Yes, that one's for you."

"It's beautiful," Steve whispered, but he didn't move, and Wilson heard him sniff slightly. "No one in the history of the world has ever told anyone how much they are loved in a more beautiful way." Steve sniffed again, but still didn't move. "And I've never felt more loved by anyone in my life." Steve still didn't move, and Wilson set down his guitar. He stood up and moved closer, and finally Steve moved into his arms. They held each other tight, standing on Wilson's front porch, and Wilson had never felt anything so right in his life. It didn't matter if anyone saw them, and it didn't matter what anyone else thought. Steve loved him, Wilson knew that, and he could feel it with every breath and every heartbeat.

"I almost lost you," Wilson whispered softly enough that he could barely hear his own voice. "I don't ever want that to happen again."

"It won't, not if I can help it," Steve said from where his head rested against Wilson's shoulder. "I'll stay with you for as long as you'll have me." Steve lifted his head, and their eyes met. "You saved my life, and not only that, you gave me hope, a place to live, and then you turned that place to live into a home. I owe you more than I can ever imagine."

Wilson shook his head slowly. "You owe me nothing. Whatever you feel you might have owed was paid back a long time ago. You're the kindest and most caring person I've ever met, and I'm damned lucky to have you in my life." Wilson leaned down, meeting Steve's lips as a cool breeze rustled the grass, blowing across the open porch. "I think we better go inside. Maria will have dinner ready soon, and if you're up to it, I'd like to show you just how much you mean to me later tonight." Steve slipped away and took Wilson's hand, leading him inside.

Dinner was indeed ready a short while later, and afterward, Wilson and Steve took a quiet evening walk around the property. They passed Steve's old truck, still parked where he'd left it after arriving. "You know, we should get you a new truck and find a good home for this one," Wilson said as he ran his hand down the side of the old rust bucket, remembering how it had run out of gas. "Maybe not," he said, changing his mind. "We'll keep this one—after all, it brought you to me."

Steve chuckled and took his hand. They walked through the barn, stroking noses as they greeted each of the horses. "I need to send Chester and Lilly back to Wally and Dakota soon. They're coming along very well. I was wondering if you'd mind if I opened a training school."

"You can do whatever you'd like. I sort of thought you'd like to breed and raise horses, but if you want to train them, that's perfectly fine as well." Wilson placed his arm around Steve's waist and guided him into the house. He knew there would be rough patches, and there were plenty of unknowns ahead, but they were happy, and that was what mattered.

Epilogue

WILSON PACED in the dressing room of the first stop on his concert tour. In the past year, he'd filmed his part in the movie, and they'd recorded their album with all of Wilson's new songs. The release had been a few days earlier, and now Willie Meadows and the band were set to perform all those songs in front of a live audience for the first time. Howard had come through big-time from a support and contract perspective. He'd managed to book him on *The Oranda Show*, where he'd found a receptive and supportive audience for telling the world he was gay. By and large, things had worked out better than he'd ever hoped, and many times he'd wondered why he'd hidden for so long.

"You look great," Howard said as Wilson fussed with his shirt for the millionth time. "But I still think you should wear the jacket. It's sort of a trademark."

Wilson picked up the leather jacket and then set it aside again. "No. That's part of who I was, and this whole tour is about letting everyone see the real me." He heard a soft knock and then the door opened. Steve walked inside carrying a large box and closed the door after him.

"I brought you something," Steve said, setting the box on the dressing table. He opened it and pulled out an old cowboy hat. "I found this at a thrift store back home. I had it cleaned, but it's old and worn and the hat of a real cowboy." Steve stepped to him and placed it on his head. Wilson looked in the mirror and smiled. The hat was perfect. "I know you're going to be great." Steve moved closer and embraced him. Wilson saw Howard step back and then quietly leave the room. "Are you nervous?"

"Terrified," Wilson answered as his stomach did a flip.

"You're going to be incredible. I know it." Steve kissed him hard and deep, not caring that someone might come in at any second. "There's nothing to worry about. The horses and ranch will still be there when you get home, and I'll still love you, no matter what, so I just want you to have fun."

Wilson nodded and kissed Steve again as the door opened slightly. "Three minutes." The door closed again, and Wilson took a final kiss for luck before checking himself in the mirror. He looked exactly the way he wanted: like a real cowboy, rather than the way he had when he'd first come to Wyoming. Now he wore Wranglers and a plain shirt, with his favorite boots that he'd broken in around the ranch.

"I'll see you out there," Steve said before kissing him yet again and then hurrying out the door. Wilson waited another few seconds, and then security came to his door and escorted him to the stage. He took his place, and then the band began to play, the lights coming up around him. He was already miked, so at his cue, he began to sing, and the crowd went wild. He waited for the crowd to settle before continuing the song. With all the lights, he couldn't really see much past the stage, but he could hear every one of the audience of twenty thousand that filled the massive concert hall. The crowd settled as he sang, and then screamed almost deafeningly when he finished.

"Thank you!" Willie said standing at the edge of the stage. "This is a new one!"

The band began to play the full-on rendition of "Walking Away from Me." As he was singing, the lighting shifted, and Wilson could see Steve standing near the stage, beaming up at him. The lights shifted again and he was gone, but it was enough to know he was there, and Willie sang the first song he'd written for Steve with all the energy and showmanship he could muster, and the crowd showed their appreciation so enthusiastically Willie could feel the building vibrate through his feet. "That song was inspired by someone very special." Another yell went through the crowd and then quieted. "Now what we just played is the version the record company liked. But there's another one. Would you like to hear it?" Willie took the crowd's enthusiasm as a yes. He motioned toward the side of the stage, and one of the men came on stage carrying a guitar and a stool. A microphone was placed near the guitar, and Willie settled. The lights on the stage dimmed and narrowed until he sat in a pool of light on an otherwise silent stage. Then he began to play.

It was just Willie and his guitar, singing the song he'd written as he'd watched Steve all those months ago. "I watch you every day, taking care of all I see, but the one thing I want most, can it ever be? Do you love me, do you need me, is it destiny? Or am I meant to only ever see your long legs walking away from me? Walking away, walking away, walking away from me." The last chord died away, and the hall was silent. Wilson waited a second and then stood up, figuring the rendition wasn't what they wanted.

Then the concert hall erupted in the loudest sound Wilson had ever heard. The entire building shook as everyone clapped, yelled, and jumped up and down. It looked like a sea of people moving and undulating as the sound continued. Once it died down, Willie commented, "So the record company was wrong?" And the sound began again.

BY THE time the concert was nearly over, Wilson was both exhilarated and exhausted. Performing always did that for him. The crowds gave him energy, but it took a great deal to entertain twenty thousand people. By the time the last note of the last song faded away and Willie had taken his final bow, he could barely stand any more. The trek to the dressing room seemed amazingly long, and he collapsed in a chair as soon as he arrived. There were drinks on the desk, and Wilson blindly reached for one. Willie Meadows was done for the night, and now it was just him. Wilson expected the usual parade of people that always stopped by after a concert, so he drank the Diet Coke in a few gulps and waited.

Howard was the first to rush in. "I've already been on the phone, and they're going to release your version of 'Walking Away From Me' as a single. It seems you proved your point."

Wilson nodded and gave Howard a smile as the band members came in, all smiles and energy.

"Looks like we did it again. They loved the new stuff," Freed said as he pulled Wilson into a hug. "And did you see all the guys in the audience? We never had that many men before." Wilson smiled and nodded. Since he'd come out, the demographic of his listeners had changed somewhat. The women still listened, and they'd picked up a lot of gay listeners, as well. It was pretty cool.

"Did you hear that crowd?" Peter asked as he nearly bounced off the walls. "That was awesome!" He high-fived Hammer, and they both laughed and grinned their happy, almost boyishly excited smiles.

"Let's hope it stays that way," Wilson said. "We have nine more cities and almost twenty concerts to go." Then he could return to the ranch for some peace and quiet. He'd only been gone a week or so and already he missed it. He'd trade the roar of the crowd for the sounds of stomping horses and the crickets at night any day.

The guys were stoked, and they hurried off to have some fun, probably at a local bar where there were plenty of women they could impress. As they left, Steve poked his head around the corner. Wilson smiled, and Steve came forward. Wilson stood and pulled him into a hug. "You were amazing," Steve whispered into Wilson's ear, tightening the hug, and everything else slipped away—the fatigue, the exhaustion, all of it seemed to leave him. "How much longer do you need to stay?"

"We can go anytime," Wilson said, and he looked around the dressing room, surprised to find that they were alone. "They'll be getting everything ready for tomorrow's concert, and then I can do it all again." Touring was like that. A couple of days in one location, and then you moved on. The show was the same, but performing night after night was wearing. "When are you scheduled to go back?"

"I'll be in here until you leave. Then I go home to wait for you," Steve told him. "Let's get you out of here and back to the hotel." Steve took his hand and led him out of the dressing room and through the people working and hanging around. Security met them and escorted the two of them to a waiting limousine that took them to their hotel.

In their room, the last of Wilson's energy failed him, and he collapsed onto the bed. Steve lay down next to him, and Wilson moved into his arms. Being held for a while felt wonderful. "What am I going to do for the rest of the tour when you're at home?"

Steve chuckled softly. "You'll think of us and know that we're waiting for you. Maria has promised your favorite dinner, and by the time you get there, the addition will be done and we can christen our huge new master bedroom." Steve nuzzled behind Wilson's ear. "I had a talk with the contractor and arranged a special surprise for you."

Wilson turned. "What kind of surprise?" He lifted his head and peered into Steve's gorgeous eyes, wishing he didn't have to leave or that Steve could stay with him, but neither was possible right now.

"You'll find out when you get home," Steve told him.

Wilson would have tried to get it out of him, but he was too tired, so instead he closed his eyes and lay in Steve's arms, the warmth of their bodies mingling, Steve's soft breath in his ear, thoughts of riding his horse and spending time on the porch playing music, the quiet and peacefulness working into him. The scene in his mind shifted, and he imagined lying in their large bed, the house open, the sounds of the night drifting in through the windows as he waited for his lover. He could hear his footsteps coming down the hall. Then Steve's shadow filled the doorway, and Wilson saw him naked, wanting him, and this time, those long legs walked toward him.

ANDREW GREY grew up in western Michigan with a father who loved to tell stories and a mother who loved to read them. Since then he has lived throughout the country and traveled throughout the world. He has a master's degree from the University of Wisconsin-Milwaukee and works in information systems for a large corporation. Andrew's hobbies include collecting antiques, gardening, and leaving his dirty dishes anywhere but in the sink (particularly when writing). He considers himself blessed with an accepting family, fantastic friends, and the world's most supportive and loving partner. Andrew currently lives in beautiful historic Carlisle, Pennsylvania.

Visit Andrew's web site at http://www.andrewgreybooks.com and blog at http://andrewgreybooks.livejournal.com/. E-mail him at andrewgrey@com cast.net.

The RANGE stories

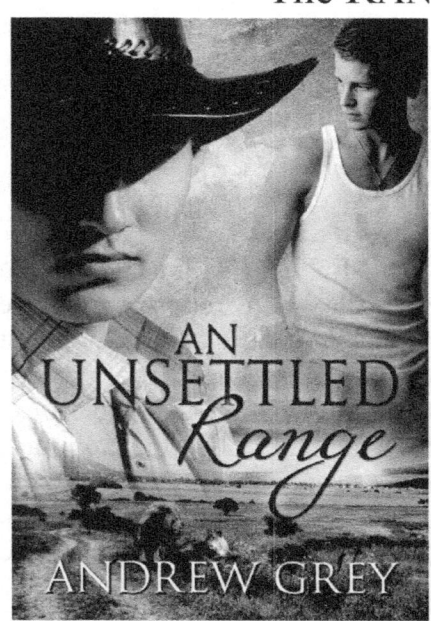

http://www.dreamspinnerpress.com

The RANGE stories

http://www.dreamspinnerpress.com

THE
GOOD
FIGHT

ANDREW GREY

THE
FIGHT
WITHIN

ANDREW GREY

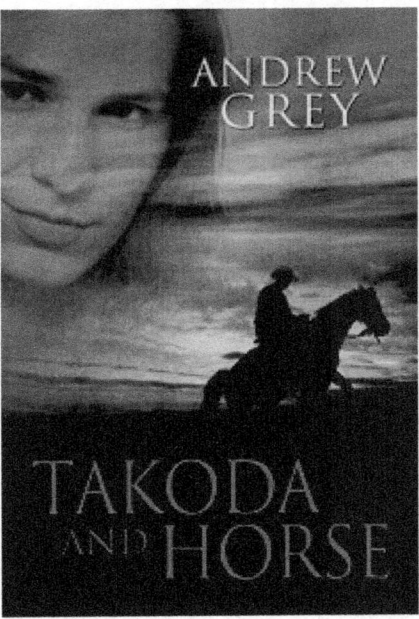

ANDREW
GREY

TAKODA
AND HORSE

THE
FIGHT FOR
IDENTITY

ANDREW
GREY

http://www.dreamspinnerpress.com

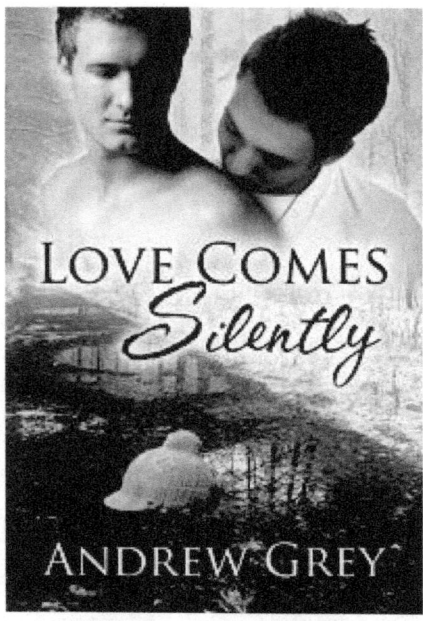

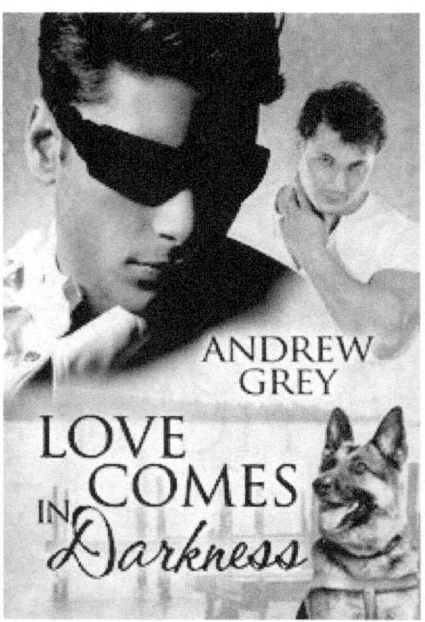

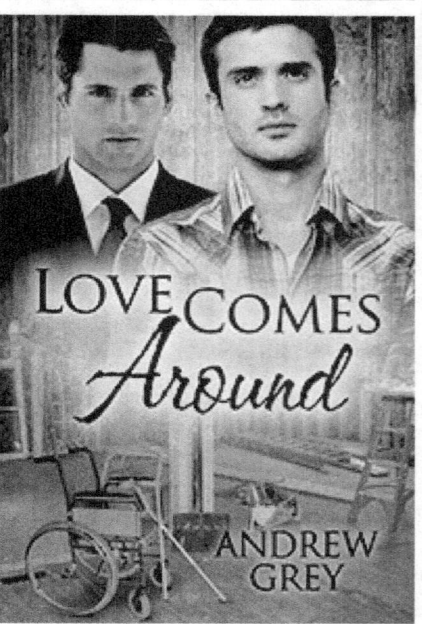

http://www.dreamspinnerpress.com

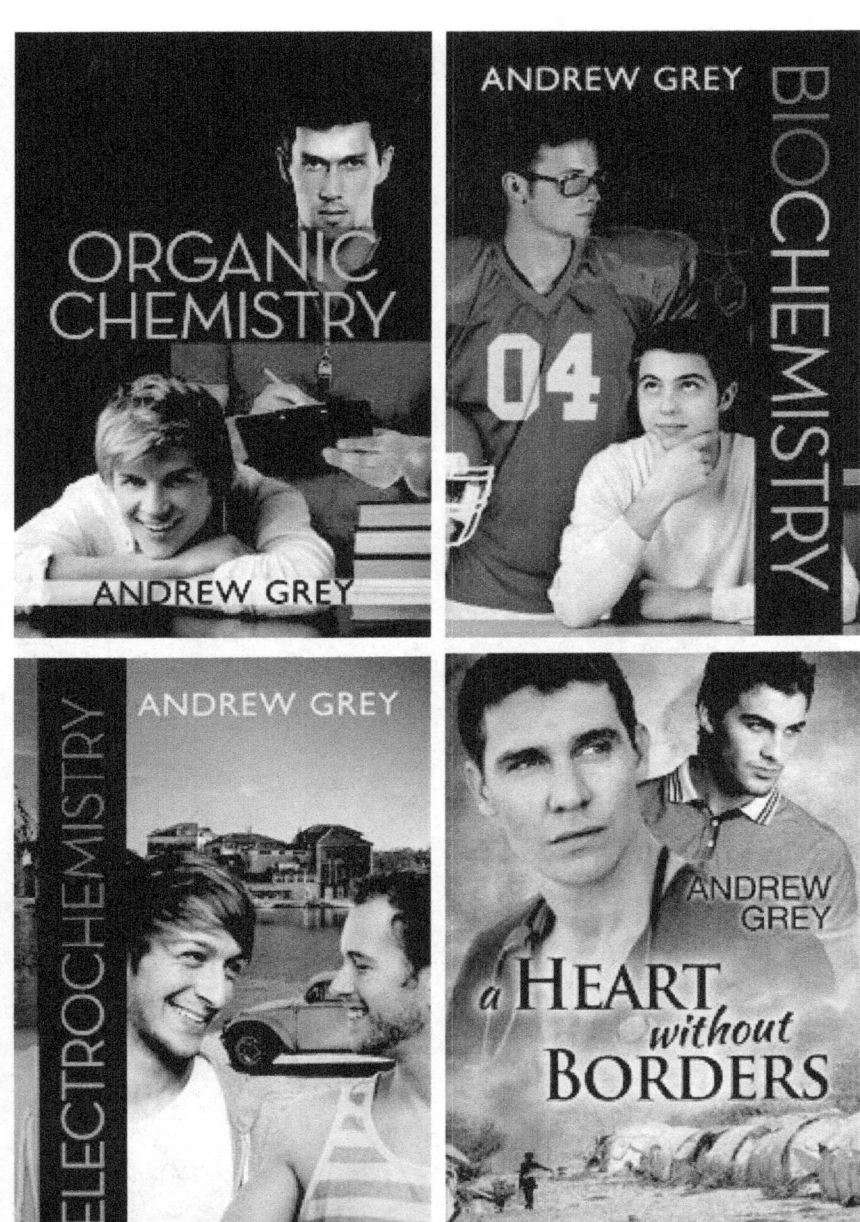

http://www.dreamspinnerpress.com

The ART stories

Now in Spanish, French, and Italian

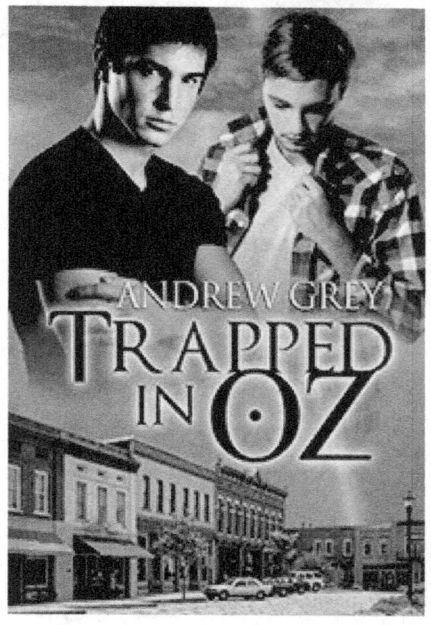

http://www.dreamspinnerpress.com

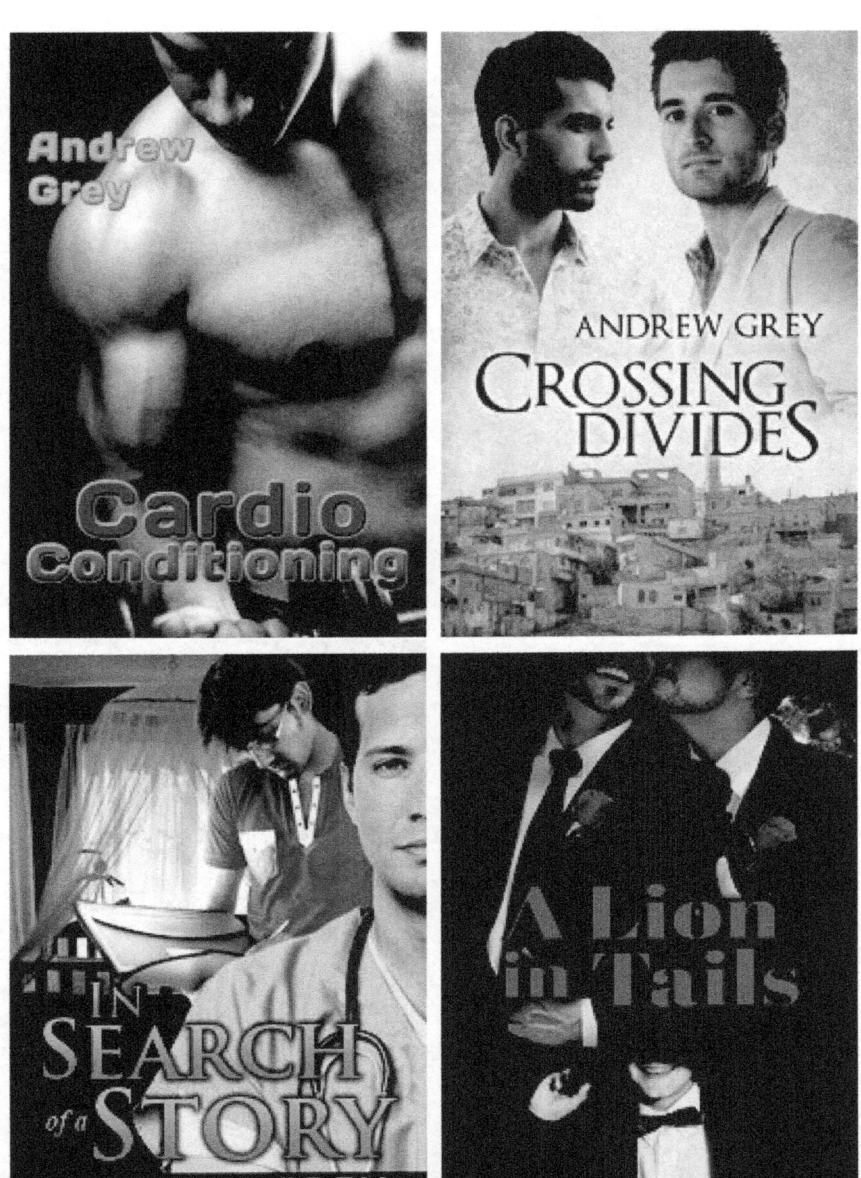

http://www.dreamspinnerpress.com

http://www.dreamspinnerpress.com

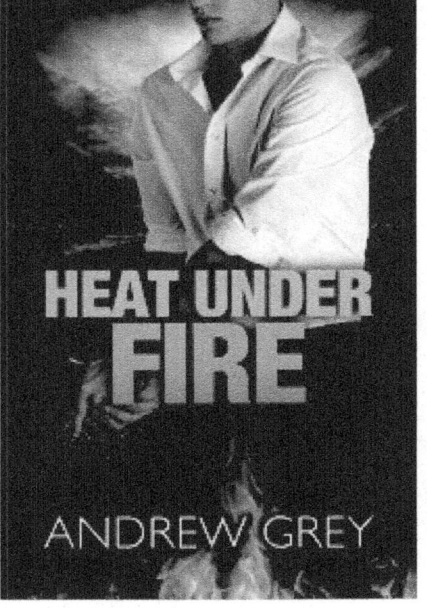

http://www.dreamspinnerpress.com

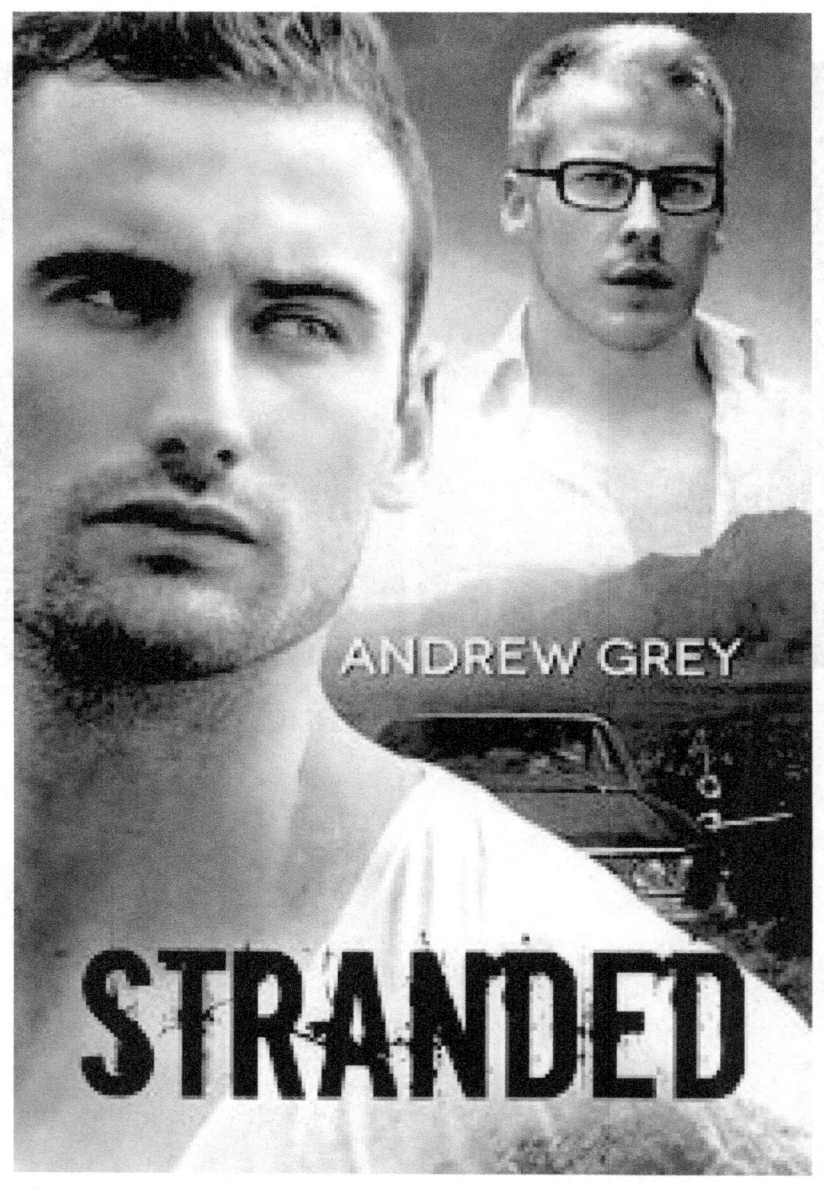

ANDREW GREY

STRANDED

http://www.dreamspinnerpress.com

TAKEN

ANDREW GREY

http://www.dreamspinnerpress.com

The LOVE MEANS... stories

http://www.dreamspinnerpress.com

FOR

MORE

OF THE

BEST

GAY

ROMANCE

Dreamspinner Press

DREAMSPINNERPRESS.COM